They and I

They and I

Jerome K. Jerome

MINT EDITIONS

They and I was first published in 1909.

This edition published by Mint Editions 2021.

ISBN 9781513278599 | E-ISBN 9781513279053

Published by Mint Editions®

 **MINT
EDITIONS**

minteditionbooks.com

Publishing Director: Jennifer Newens
Design & Production: Rachel Lopez Metzger
Project Manager: Micaela Clark
Typesetting: Westchester Publishing Services

CONTENTS

I

I t is not a large house," I said. "We don't want a large house. Two spare bedrooms, and the little three-cornered place you see marked there on the plan, next to the bathroom, and which will just do for a bachelor, will be all we shall require—at all events, for the present. Later on, if I ever get rich, we can throw out a wing. The kitchen I shall have to break to your mother gently. Whatever the original architect could have been thinking of—"

"Never mind the kitchen," said Dick: "what about the billiard-room?"

The way children nowadays will interrupt a parent is nothing short of a national disgrace. I also wish Dick would not sit on the table, swinging his legs. It is not respectful. "Why, when I was a boy," as I said to him, "I should as soon have thought of sitting on a table, interrupting my father—"

"What's this thing in the middle of the hall, that looks like a grating?" demanded Robina.

"She means the stairs," explained Dick.

"Then why don't they look like stairs?" commented Robina.

"They do," replied Dick, "to people with sense."

"They don't," persisted Robina, "they look like a grating." Robina, with the plan spread out across her knee, was sitting balanced on the arm of an easy-chair. Really, I hardly see the use of buying chairs for these people. Nobody seems to know what they are for—except it be one or another of the dogs. Perches are all they want.

"If we threw the drawing-room into the hall and could do away with the stairs," thought Robina, "we should be able to give a dance now and then."

"Perhaps," I suggested, "you would like to clear out the house altogether, leaving nothing but the four bare walls. That would give us still more room, that would. For just living in, we could fix up a shed in the garden; or—"

"I'm talking seriously," said Robina: "what's the good of a drawing-room? One only wants it to show the sort of people into that one wishes hadn't come. They'd sit about, looking miserable, just as well anywhere else. If we could only get rid of the stairs—"

"Oh, of course! we could get rid of the stairs," I agreed. "It would be a bit awkward at first, when we wanted to go to bed. But I daresay we should get used to it. We could have a ladder and climb up to our rooms through the windows. Or we might adopt the Norwegian method and have the stairs outside."

"I wish you would be sensible," said Robin.

"I am trying to be," I explained; "and I am also trying to put a little sense into you. At present you are crazy about dancing. If you had your way, you would turn the house into a dancing-saloon with primitive sleeping-accommodation attached. It will last six months, your dancing craze. Then you will want the house transformed into a swimming-bath, or a skating-rink, or cleared out for hockey. My idea may be conventional. I don't expect you to sympathise with it. My notion is just an ordinary Christian house, not a gymnasium. There are going to be bedrooms in this house, and there's going to be a staircase leading to them. It may strike you as sordid, but there is also going to be a kitchen: though why when building the house they should have put the kitchen—"

"Don't forget the billiard-room," said Dick.

"If you thought more of your future career and less about billiards," Robin pointed out to him, "perhaps you'd get through your Little-go in the course of the next few years. If Pa only had sense—I mean if he wasn't so absurdly indulgent wherever you are concerned, he would not have a billiard-table in the house."

"You talk like that," retorted Dick, "merely because you can't play."

"I can beat you, anyhow," retorted Robin.

"Once," admitted Dick—"once in six weeks."

"Twice," corrected Robin.

"You don't play," Dick explained to her; "you just whack round and trust to Providence."

"I don't whack round," said Robin; "I always aim at something. When you try and it doesn't come off, you say it's 'hard luck;' and when I try and it does come off, you say it's fluking. So like a man."

"You both of you," I said, "attach too much importance to the score. When you try for a cannon off the white and hit it on the wrong side and send it into a pocket, and your own ball travels on and makes a losing hazard off the red, instead of being vexed with yourselves—"

"If you get a really good table, governor," said Dick, "I'll teach you billiards."

I do believe Dick really thinks he can play. It is the same with golf. Beginners are invariably lucky. "I think I shall like it," they tell you; "I seem to have the game in me, if you understand."

'There is a friend of mine, an old sea-captain. He is the sort of man that when the three balls are lying in a straight line, tucked up under the cushion, looks pleased; because then he knows he can make a cannon and leave the red just where he wants it. An Irish youngster named Malooney, a college chum of Dick's, was staying with us; and the afternoon being wet, the Captain said he would explain it to Malooney, how a young man might practise billiards without any danger of cutting the cloth. He taught him how to hold the cue, and he told him how to make a bridge. Malooney was grateful, and worked for about an hour. He did not show much promise. He is a powerfully built young man, and he didn't seem able to get it into his head that he wasn't playing cricket. Whenever he hit a little low the result was generally lost ball. To save time—and damage to furniture—Dick and I fielded for him. Dick stood at long-stop, and I was short slip. It was dangerous work, however, and when Dick had caught him out twice running, we agreed that we had won, and took him in to tea. In the evening—none of the rest of us being keen to try our luck a second time—the Captain said, that just for the joke of the thing he would give Malooney eighty-five and play him a hundred up. To confess the truth, I find no particular fun myself in playing billiards with the Captain. The game consists, as far as I am concerned, in walking round the table, throwing him back the balls, and saying "Good!" By the time my turn comes I don't seem to care what happens: everything seems against me. He is a kind old gentleman and he means well, but the tone in which he says "Hard lines!" whenever I miss an easy stroke irritates me. I feel I'd like to throw the balls at his head and fling the table out of window. I suppose it is that I am in a fretful state of mind, but the mere way in which he chalks his cue aggravates me. He carries his own chalk in his waistcoat pocket—as if our chalk wasn't good enough for him—and when he has finished chalking, he smooths the tip round with his finger and thumb and taps the cue against the table. "Oh! go on with the game," I want to say to him; "don't be so full of tricks."

THE CAPTAIN LED OFF WITH a miss in baulk. Malooney gripped his cue, drew in a deep breath, and let fly. The result was ten: a cannon and all three balls in the same pocket. As a matter of fact he made the cannon twice; but the second time, as we explained to him, of course did not count.

"Good beginning!" said the Captain.

Malooney seemed pleased with himself, and took off his coat.

Malooney's ball missed the red on its first journey up the table by about a foot, but found it later on and sent it into a pocket.

"Ninety-nine plays nothing," said Dick, who was marking. "Better make it a hundred and fifty, hadn't we, Captain?"

"Well, I'd like to get in a shot," said the Captain, "before the game is over. Perhaps we had better make it a hundred and fifty, if Mr. Malooney has no objection."

"Whatever you think right, sir," said Rory Malooney.

Malooney finished his break for twenty-two, leaving himself hanging over the middle pocket and the red tucked up in baulk.

"Nothing plays a hundred and eight," said Dick.

"When I want the score," said the Captain, "I'll ask for it."

"Beg pardon, sir," said Dick.

"I hate a noisy game," said the Captain.

The Captain, making up his mind without much waste of time, sent his ball under the cushion, six inches outside baulk.

"What will I do here?" asked Malooney.

"I don't know what you will do," said the Captain; "I'm waiting to see."

Owing to the position of the ball, Malooney was unable to employ his whole strength. All he did that turn was to pocket the Captain's ball and leave himself under the bottom cushion, four inches from the red. The Captain said a nautical word, and gave another miss. Malooney squared up to the balls for the third time. They flew before him, panic-stricken. They banged against one another, came back and hit one another again for no reason whatever. The red, in particular, Malooney had succeeded apparently in frightening out of its wits. It is a stupid ball, generally speaking, our red—its one idea to get under a cushion and watch the game. With Malooney it soon found it was safe nowhere on the table. Its only hope was pockets. I may have been mistaken, my eye may have been deceived by the rapidity of the play, but it seemed to me that the red never waited to be hit. When it saw Malooney's ball coming for it at the rate of forty miles an hour, it just made for the nearest pocket. It rushed round the table looking for pockets. If in its excitement, it passed an empty pocket, it turned back and crawled in. There were times when in its terror it jumped the table and took shelter under the sofa or behind the sideboard. One began to feel sorry for the red.

The Captain had scored a legitimate thirty-eight, and Malooney had given him twenty-four, when it really seemed as if the Captain's chance had come. I could have scored myself as the balls were then.

"Sixty-two plays one hundred and twenty-eight. Now then, Captain, game in your hands," said Dick.

We gathered round. The children left their play. It was a pretty picture: the bright young faces, eager with expectation, the old worn veteran squinting down his cue, as if afraid that watching Malooney's play might have given it the squirms.

"Now follow this," I whispered to Malooney. "Don't notice merely what he does, but try and understand why he does it. Any fool—after a little practice, that is—can hit a ball. But why do you hit it? What happens after you've hit it? What—"

"Hush," said Dick.

The Captain drew his cue back and gently pushed it forward.

"Pretty stroke," I whispered to Malooney; "now, that's the sort—"

I offer, by way of explanation, that the Captain by this time was probably too full of bottled-up language to be master of his nerves. The ball travelled slowly past the red. Dick said afterwards that you couldn't have put so much as a sheet of paper between them. It comforts a man, sometimes, when you tell him this; and at other times it only makes him madder. It travelled on and passed the white—you could have put quite a lot of paper between it and the white—and dropped with a contented thud into the top left-hand pocket.

"Why does he do that?" Malooney whispered. Malooney has a singularly hearty whisper.

Dick and I got the women and children out of the room as quickly as we could, but of course Veronica managed to tumble over something on the way—Veronica would find something to tumble over in the desert of Sahara; and a few days later I overheard expressions, scorching their way through the nursery door, that made my hair rise up. I entered, and found Veronica standing on the table. Jumbo was sitting upon the music-stool. The poor dog himself was looking scared, though he must have heard a bit of language in his time, one way and another.

"Veronica," I said, "are you not ashamed of yourself? You wicked child, how dare you—"

"It's all right," said Veronica. "I don't really mean any harm. He's a sailor, and I have to talk to him like that, else he don't know he's being talked to."

I pay hard-working, conscientious ladies to teach this child things right and proper for her to know. They tell her clever things that Julius Cæsar said; observations made by Marcus Aurelius that, pondered over, might help her to become a beautiful character. She complains that it produces a strange buzzy feeling in her head; and her mother argues that perhaps her brain is of the creative order, not intended to remember much—thinks that perhaps she is going to be something. A good round-dozen oaths the Captain must have let fly before Dick and I succeeded in rolling her out of the room. She had only heard them once, yet, so far as I could judge, she had got them letter perfect.

The Captain, now no longer under the necessity of employing all his energies to suppress his natural instincts, gradually recovered form, and eventually the game stood at one hundred and forty-nine all, Malooney to play. The Captain had left the balls in a position that would have disheartened any other opponent than Malooney. To any other opponent than Malooney the Captain would have offered irritating sympathy. "Afraid the balls are not rolling well for you to-night," the Captain would have said; or, "Sorry, sir, I don't seem to have left you very much." To-night the Captain wasn't feeling playful.

"Well, if he scores off that!" said Dick.

"Short of locking up the balls and turning out the lights, I don't myself see how one is going to stop him," sighed the Captain.

The Captain's ball was in hand. Malooney went for the red and hit—perhaps it would be more correct to say, frightened—it into a pocket. Malooney's ball, with the table to itself, then gave a solo performance, and ended up by breaking a window. It was what the lawyers call a nice point. What was the effect upon the score?

Malooney argued that, seeing he had pocketed the red before his own ball left the table, his three should be counted first, and that therefore he had won. Dick maintained that a ball that had ended up in a flower-bed couldn't be deemed to have scored anything. The Captain declined to assist. He said that, although he had been playing billiards for upwards of forty years, the incident was new to him. My own feeling was that of thankfulness that we had got through the game without anybody being really injured. We agreed that the person to decide the point would be the editor of *The Field*.

It remains still undecided. The Captain came into my study the next morning. He said: "If you haven't written that letter to *The Field*, don't mention my name. They know me on *The Field*. I would rather it did not get about that I have been playing with a man who cannot keep his ball within the four walls of a billiard-room."

"Well," I answered, "I know most of the fellows on *The Field* myself.

They don't often get hold of anything novel in the way of a story. When they do, they are apt to harp upon it. My idea was to keep my own name out of it altogether."

"It is not a point likely to crop up often," said the Captain. "I'd let it rest if I were you."

I should like to have had it settled. In the end, I wrote the editor a careful letter, in a disguised hand, giving a false name and address. But if any answer ever appeared I must have missed it.

Myself I have a sort of consciousness that somewhere inside me there is quite a good player, if only I could persuade him to come out. He is shy, that is all. He does not seem able to play when people are looking on. The shots he misses when people are looking on would give you a wrong idea of him. When nobody is about, a prettier game you do not often see. If some folks who fancy themselves could see me when there is nobody about, it might take the conceit out of them. Only once I played up to what I feel is my real form, and then it led to argument. I was staying at an hotel in Switzerland, and the second evening a pleasant-spoken young fellow, who said he had read all my books—later, he appeared surprised on learning I had written more than two—asked me if I would care to play a hundred up. We played even, and I paid for the table. The next evening he said he thought it would make a better game if he gave me forty and I broke. It was a fairly close finish, and afterwards he suggested that I should put down my name for the handicap they were arranging.

"I am afraid," I answered, "that I hardly play well enough. Just a quiet game with you is one thing; but in a handicap with a crowd looking on—"

"I should not let that trouble you," he said; "there are some here who play worse than you—just one or two. It passes the evening."

It was merely a friendly affair. I paid my twenty marks, and was given plus a hundred. I drew for my first game a chatty type of man, who started minus twenty. We neither of us did much for the first five minutes, and then I made a break of forty-four.

There was not a fluke in it from beginning to end. I was never more astonished in my life. It seemed to me it was the cue was doing it.

Minus Twenty was even more astonished. I heard him as I passed:

"Who handicapped this man?" he asked.

"I did," said the pleasant-spoken youngster.

"Oh," said Minus Twenty—"friend of yours, I presume?"

There are evenings that seem to belong to you. We finished that two hundred and fifty under the three-quarters of an hour. I explained to Minus Twenty—he was plus sixty-three at the end—that my play that night had been exceptional. He said that he had heard of cases similar. I left him talking volubly to the committee. He was not a nice man at all.

After that I did not care to win; and that of course was fatal. The less I tried, the more impossible it seemed for me to do wrong. I was left in at the last with a man from another hotel. But for that I am convinced I should have carried off the handicap. Our hotel didn't, anyhow, want the other hotel to win. So they gathered round me, and offered me sound advice, and begged me to be careful; with the natural result that I went back to my usual form quite suddenly.

Never before or since have I played as I played that week. But it showed me what I could do. I shall get a new table, with proper pockets this time. There is something wrong about our pockets. The balls go into them and then come out again. You would think they had seen something there to frighten them. They come out trembling and hold on to the cushion.

I shall also get a new red ball. I fancy it must be a very old ball, our red. It seems to me to be always tired.

"The billiard-room," I said to Dick, "I see my way to easily enough. Adding another ten feet to what is now the dairy will give us twenty-eight by twenty. I am hopeful that will be sufficient even for your friend Malooney. The drawing-room is too small to be of any use. I may decide—as Robina has suggested—to 'throw it into the hall.' But the stairs will remain. For dancing, private theatricals—things to keep you children out of mischief—I have an idea I will explain to you later on. The kitchen—"

"Can I have a room to myself?" asked Veronica.

Veronica was sitting on the floor, staring into the fire, her chin supported by her hand. Veronica, in those rare moments when she is resting from her troubles, wears a holy, far-away expression apt to mislead the stranger. Governesses, new to her, have their doubts whether on these occasions they are justified in dragging her back to discuss mere dates and tables. Poets who are friends of mine, coming unexpectedly upon Veronica standing by the window, gazing upward at the evening star, have thought it was a vision, until they got closer and found that she was sucking peppermints.

"I should so like to have a room all to myself," added Veronica.

"It would be a room!" commented Robin.

"It wouldn't have your hairpins sticking up all over the bed, anyhow," murmured Veronica dreamily.

"I like that!" said Robin; "why—"

"You're harder than I am," said Veronica.

"I should wish you to have a room, Veronica," I said. "My fear is that in place of one untidy bedroom in the house—a room that makes me shudder every time I see it through the open door; and the door, in spite of all I can say, generally is wide open—"

"I'm not untidy," said Robin, "not really. I know where everything is in the dark—if people would only leave them alone."

"You are. You're about the most untidy girl I know," said Dick.

"I'm not," said Robin; "you don't see other girls' rooms. Look at yours at Cambridge. Malooney told us you'd had a fire, and we all believed him at first."

"When a man's working—" said Dick.

"He must have an orderly place to work in," suggested Robin.

Dick sighed. "It's never any good talking to you," said Dick. "You don't even see your own faults."

"I can," said Robin; "I see them more than anyone. All I claim is justice."

"Show me, Veronica," I said, "that you are worthy to possess a room. At present you appear to regard the whole house as your room. I find your gaiters on the croquet lawn. A portion of your costume—an article that anyone possessed of the true feelings of a lady would desire to keep hidden from the world—is discovered waving from the staircase window."

"I put it out to be mended," explained Veronica.

"You opened the door and flung it out. I told you of it at the time," said Robin. "You do the same with your boots."

"You are too high-spirited for your size," explained Dick to her. "Try to be less dashing."

"I could also wish, Veronica," I continued, "that you shed your back comb less easily, or at least that you knew when you had shed it. As for your gloves—well, hunting your gloves has come to be our leading winter sport."

"People look in such funny places for them," said Veronica.

"Granted. But be just, Veronica," I pleaded. "Admit that it is in funny places we occasionally find them. When looking for your things one learns, Veronica, never to despair. So long as there remains a corner unexplored inside or outside the house, within the half-mile radius, hope need not be abandoned."

Veronica was still gazing dreamily into the fire.

"I suppose," said Veronica, "it's reditty."

"It's what?" I said.

"She means heredity," suggested Dick—"cheeky young beggar! I wonder you let her talk to you the way she does."

"Besides," added Robin, "as I am always explaining to you, Pa is a literary man. With him it is part of his temperament."

"It's hard on us children," said Veronica.

We were all agreed—with the exception of Veronica—that it was time Veronica went to bed. As chairman I took it upon myself to closure the debate.

II

D o you mean, Governor, that you have actually bought the house?"
demanded Dick, "or are we only talking about it?"

"This time, Dick," I answered, "I have done it."

Dick looked serious. "Is it what you wanted?" he asked.

"No, Dick," I replied, "it is not what I wanted. I wanted an old-fashioned, picturesque, rambling sort of a place, all gables and ivy and oriel windows."

"You are mixing things up," Dick interrupted, "gables and oriel windows don't go together."

"I beg your pardon, Dick," I corrected him, "in the house I wanted, they do. It is the style of house you find in the Christmas number. I have never seen it anywhere else, but I took a fancy to it from the first. It is not too far from the church, and it lights up well at night. 'One of these days,' I used to say to myself when a boy, 'I'll be a clever man and live in a house just like that.' It was my dream."

"And what is this place like?" demanded Robin, "this place you have bought."

"The agent," I explained, "claims for it that it is capable of improvement. I asked him to what school of architecture he would say it belonged; he said he thought that it must have been a local school, and pointed out—what seems to be the truth—that nowadays they do not build such houses."

"Near to the river?" demanded Dick.

"Well, by the road," I answered, "I daresay it may be a couple of miles."

"And by the shortest way?" questioned Dick.

"That is the shortest way," I explained; "there's a prettier way through the woods, but that is about three miles and a half."

"But we had decided it was to be near the river," said Robin.

"We also decided," I replied, "that it was to be on sandy soil, with a south-west aspect. Only one thing in this house has a south-west aspect, and that's the back door. I asked the agent about the sand. He advised me, if I wanted it in any quantity, to get an estimate from the Railway Company. I wanted it on a hill. It is on a hill, with a bigger hill in front of it. I didn't want that other hill. I wanted an uninterrupted view of the southern half of England. I wanted to take people out on the step, and cram them with stories about our being able on clear days to see the Bristol Channel. They might not have believed me, but without that hill I could have stuck to it, and they could not have been certain—not dead certain—I was lying.

"Personally, I should have liked a house where something had happened. I should have liked, myself, a blood-stain—not a fussy blood-stain, a neat unobtrusive blood-stain that would have been content, most of its time, to remain hidden under the mat, shown only occasionally as a treat to visitors. I had hopes even of a ghost. I don't mean one of those noisy ghosts that doesn't seem to know it is dead. A lady ghost would have been my fancy, a gentle ghost with quiet, pretty ways. This house—well, it is such a sensible-looking house, that is my chief objection to it. It has got an echo. If you go to the end of the garden and shout at it very loudly, it answers you back. This is the only bit of fun you can have with it. Even then it answers you in such a tone you feel it thinks the whole thing silly—is doing it merely to humour you. It is one of those houses that always seems to be thinking of its rates and taxes."

"Any reason at all for your having bought it?" asked Dick.

"Yes, Dick," I answered. "We are all of us tired of this suburb. We want to live in the country and be good. To live in the country with any comfort it is necessary to have a house there. This being admitted, it follows we must either build a house or buy one. I would rather not build a house. Talboys built himself a house. You know Talboys. When I first met him, before he started building, he was a cheerful soul with a kindly word for everyone. The builder assures him that in another twenty years, when the colour has had time to tone down, his house will be a picture. At present it makes him bilious, the mere sight of it. Year by year, they tell him, as the dampness wears itself away, he will suffer less and less from rheumatism, ague, and lumbago. He has a hedge round the garden; it is eighteen inches high. To keep the boys out he has put up barbed-wire fencing. But wire fencing affords no real privacy. When the Talboys are taking coffee on the lawn, there is generally a crowd from the village watching them. There are trees in the garden; you know they are trees—there is a label tied to each one telling you what sort of tree it is. For the moment there is a similarity about them. Thirty years hence, Talboys estimates, they will afford him shade and comfort; but by that time he hopes to be dead. I want a house that has got over all its troubles; I don't want to spend the rest of my life bringing up a young and inexperienced house."

"But why this particular house?" urged Robin, "if, as you say, it is not the house you wanted."

"Because, my dear girl," I answered, "it is less unlike the house I wanted than other houses I have seen. When we are young we make up our minds to try and get what we want; when we have arrived at years of discretion we decide to try and want what we can get. It saves time. During the last two years I have seen about sixty houses, and out of the lot there was only one that was really the house I wanted. Hitherto I have kept the story to myself. Even now, thinking about it irritates me. It was not an agent who told me of it. I met a man by chance in a railway carriage. He had a black eye. If ever I meet him again I'll give him another. He accounted for it by explaining that he had had trouble with a golf ball, and at the time I believed him. I mentioned to him in conversation I was looking for a house. He described this place to me, and it seemed to me hours before the train stopped at a station. When it did I got out and took the next train back. I did not even wait for lunch. I had my bicycle with me, and I went straight there. It was—well, it was the house I wanted. If it had vanished suddenly, and I had found myself in bed, the whole thing would have seemed more reasonable. The proprietor opened the door to me himself. He had the bearing of a retired military man. It was afterwards I learnt he was the proprietor.

"I said, 'Good afternoon; if it is not troubling you, I would like to look over the house.' We were standing in the oak-panelled hall. I noticed the carved staircase about which the man in the train had told me, also the Tudor fireplaces. That is all I had time to notice. The next moment I was lying on my back in the middle of the gravel with the door shut. I looked up. I saw the old maniac's head sticking out of a little window. It was an evil face. He had a gun in his hand.

"'I'm going to count twenty,' he said. 'If you are not the other side of the gate by then, I shoot.'

"I ran over the figures myself on my way to the gate. I made it eighteen.

"I had an hour to wait for the train. I talked the matter over with the station-master.

"'Yes,' he said, 'there'll be trouble up there one of these days.'

"I said, 'It seems to me to have begun.'

"He said, 'It's the Indian sun. It gets into their heads. We have one or two in the neighbourhood. They are quiet enough till something happens.'

"'If I'd been two seconds longer,' I said, 'I believe he'd have done it.'

"'It's a taking house,' said the station-master; 'not too big and not too little. It's the sort of house people seem to be looking for.'

"'I don't envy,' I said, 'the next person that finds it.'

"'He settled himself down here,' said the station-master, 'about ten years ago. Since then, if one person has offered to take the house off his hands, I suppose a thousand have. At first he would laugh at them good-temperedly—explain to them that his idea was to live there himself, in peace and quietness, till he died. Two out of every three of them would express their willingness to wait for that, and suggest some arrangement by which they might enter into possession, say, a week after the funeral. The last few months it has been worse than ever. I reckon you're about the eighth that has been up there this week, and to-day only Thursday. There's something to be said, you know, for the old man.'"

"And did he," asked Dick—"did he shoot the next party that came along?"

"Don't be so silly, Dick," said Robin; "it's a story. Tell us another, Pa."

"I don't know what you mean, Robina, by a story," I said. "If you mean to imply—"

Robina said she didn't; but I know quite well she did. Because I am an author, and have to tell stories for my living, people think I don't know any truth. It is vexing enough to be doubted when one is exaggerating; to have sneers flung at one by one's own kith and kin when one is struggling to confine oneself to bald, bare narrative—well, where is the inducement to be truthful? There are times when I almost say to myself that I will never tell the truth again.

"As it happens," I said, "the story is true, in many places. I pass over your indifference to the risk I ran; though a nice girl at the point where the gun was mentioned would have expressed alarm. Anyhow, at the end you might have said something more sympathetic than merely, 'Tell us another.' He did not shoot the next party that arrived, for the reason that the very next day his wife, alarmed at what had happened, went up to London and consulted an expert—none too soon, as it turned out. The poor old fellow died six months later in a private lunatic asylum; I had it from the station-master on passing through the junction again this spring. The house fell into the possession of his nephew, who is living in it now. He is a youngish man with a large family, and people have learnt that the place is not for sale. It seems to me rather a sad story. The Indian sun, as the station-master thinks, may have started the trouble; but the end was undoubtedly hastened by the annoyance to which the unfortunate gentleman had been subjected; and I myself might have been shot. The only thing that comforts me is thinking of that fool's black eye—the fool that sent me there."

"And none of the other houses," suggested Dick, "were any good at all?"

"There were drawbacks, Dick," I explained. "There was a house in Essex; it was one of the first your mother and I inspected. I nearly shed tears of joy when I read the advertisement. It had once been a priory. Queen Elizabeth had slept there on her way to Greenwich. A photograph of the house accompanied the advertisement. I should not have believed the thing had it been a picture. It was under twelve miles from Charing Cross. The owner, it was stated, was open to offers."

"All humbug, I suppose," suggested Dick.

"The advertisement, if anything," I replied, "had under-estimated the attractiveness of that house. All I blame the advertisement for is that it did not mention other things. It did not mention, for instance, that since Queen Elizabeth's time the neighbourhood had changed. It did not mention that the entrance was between a public-house one side of the gate and a fried-fish shop on the other; that the Great Eastern Railway-Company had established a goods depot at the bottom of the garden; that the drawing-room windows looked out on extensive chemical works, and the dining-room windows, which were round the corner, on a stonemason's yard. The house itself was a dream."

"But what is the sense of it?" demanded Dick. "What do house agents think is the good of it? Do they think people likely to take a house after reading the advertisement without ever going to see it?"

"I asked an agent once that very question," I replied. "He said they did it first and foremost to keep up the spirits of the owner—the man who wanted to sell the house. He said that when a man was trying to part with a house he had to listen to so much abuse of it from people who came to see it that if somebody did not stick up for the house—say all that could be said for it, and gloss over its defects—he would end by becoming so ashamed of it he would want to give it away, or blow it up with dynamite. He said that reading the advertisement in the agent's catalogue was the only thing that reconciled him to being the owner of the house. He said one client of his had been trying to sell his house for years—until one day in the office he read by chance the agent's description of it. Upon which he went straight home, took down the board, and has lived there contentedly ever since. From that point of view there is reason in the system; but for the house-hunter it works badly.

"One agent sent me a day's journey to see a house standing in the middle of a brickfield, with a view of the Grand Junction Canal. I asked him where was the river he had mentioned. He explained it was the other side of the canal, but on a lower level; that was the only reason why from the house you couldn't see it. I asked him for his picturesque scenery. He explained it was farther on, round the bend. He seemed to think me unreasonable, expecting to find everything I wanted just outside the front-door. He suggested my shutting out the brickfield—if I didn't like the brickfield—with trees. He suggested the eucalyptus-tree. He said it was a rapid grower. He also told me that it yielded gum.

"Another house I travelled down into Dorsetshire to see. It contained, according to the advertisement, 'perhaps the most perfect specimen of Norman arch extant in Southern England.' It was to be found mentioned in Dugdale, and dated from the thirteenth century. I don't quite know what I expected. I argued to myself that there must have been ruffians of only moderate means even in those days. Here and there some robber baron who had struck a poor line of country would have had to be content with a homely little castle. A few such, hidden away in unfrequented districts, had escaped destruction. More civilised descendants had adapted them to later requirements. I had in my mind, before the train reached Dorchester, something between a miniature Tower of London and a mediæval edition of Ann Hathaway's cottage at Stratford. I pictured dungeons and a drawbridge, perhaps a secret passage. Lamchick has a secret passage, leading from behind a sort of portrait in the dining-room to the back of the kitchen chimney. They use it for a linen closet. It seems to me a pity. Of course originally it went on farther. The vicar, who is a bit of an antiquarian, believes it comes out somewhere in the churchyard. I tell Lamchick he ought to have it opened up, but his wife doesn't want it touched. She seems to think it just right as it is. I have always had a fancy for a secret passage. I decided I would have the drawbridge repaired and made practicable. Flanked on each side with flowers in tubs, it would have been a novel and picturesque approach."

"Was there a drawbridge?" asked Dick.

"There was no drawbridge," I explained. "The entrance to the house was through what the caretaker called the conservatory. It was not the sort of house that goes with a drawbridge."

"Then what about the Norman arches?" argued Dick.

"Not arches," I corrected him; "Arch. The Norman arch was downstairs in the kitchen. It was the kitchen, that had been built in the thirteenth century—and had not had much done to it since, apparently. Originally, I should say, it had been the torture chamber; it gave you that idea. I think your mother would have raised objections to the kitchen—anyhow, when she came to think of the cook. It would have been necessary to put it to the woman before engaging her:—

"'You don't mind cooking in a dungeon in the dark, do you?'

"Some cooks would. The rest of the house was what I should describe as present-day mixed style. The last tenant but one had thrown out a bathroom in corrugated iron."

"Then there was a house in Berkshire that I took your mother to see, with a trout stream running through the grounds. I imagined myself going out after lunch, catching trout for dinner; inviting swagger friends down to 'my little place in Berkshire' for a few days' trout-fishing. There is a man I once knew who is now a baronet. He used to be keen on fishing. I thought maybe I'd get him. It would have looked well in the Literary Gossip column: 'Among the other distinguished guests'—you know the sort of thing. I had the paragraph already in my mind. The wonder is I didn't buy a rod."

"Wasn't there any trout stream?" questioned Robin.

"There was a stream," I answered; "if anything, too much stream. The stream was the first thing your mother noticed. She noticed it a quarter of an hour before we came to it—before we knew it was the stream. We drove back to the town, and she bought a smelling-bottle, the larger size.

"It gave your mother a headache, that stream, and made me mad. The agent's office was opposite the station. I allowed myself half an hour on my way back to tell him what I thought of him, and then I missed the train. I could have got it in if he had let me talk all the time, but he would interrupt. He said it was the people at the paper-mill—that he had spoken to them about it more than once; he seemed to think sympathy was all I wanted. He assured me, on his word as a house-agent, that it had once been a trout stream. The fact was historical. Isaac Walton had fished there—that was prior to the paper-mill. He thought a collection of trout, male and female, might be bought and placed in it; preference being given to some hardy breed of trout, accustomed to roughing it. I told him I wasn't looking for a place where I could play at being Noah; and left him, as I explained to him, with the intention of going straight to my solicitors and instituting proceedings against him for talking like a fool; and he put on his hat and went across to his solicitors to commence proceedings against me for libel.

"I suppose that, with myself, he thought better of it in the end. But I'm tired of having my life turned into one perpetual first of April. This house that I have bought is not my heart's desire, but about it there are possibilities. We will put in lattice windows, and fuss-up the chimneys. Maybe we will let in a tablet over the front-door, with a date—always looks well: it is a picturesque figure, the old-fashioned five. By the time we have done with it—for all practical purposes— it will be a Tudor manor-house. I have always wanted an old Tudor manor-house. There is no reason, so far as I can see, why there should not be stories connected with this house. Why should not we have a room in which Somebody once slept? We won't have Queen Elizabeth. I'm tired of Queen Elizabeth. Besides, I don't believe she'd have been nice. Why not Queen Anne? A quiet, gentle old lady, from all accounts, who would not have given trouble. Or, better still, Shakespeare. He was constantly to and fro between London and Stratford. It would not have been so very much out of his way. 'The room where Shakespeare slept!' Why, it's a new idea. Nobody ever seems to have thought of Shakespeare. There is the four-post bedstead. Your mother never liked it. She will insist, it harbours things. We might hang the wall with scenes from his plays, and have a bust of the old gentleman himself over the door. If I'm left alone and not worried, I'll probably end by believing that he really did sleep there."

"What about cupboards?" suggested Dick. "The Little Mother will clamour for cupboards."

It is unexplainable, the average woman's passion for cupboards. In heaven, her first request, I am sure, is always, "Can I have a cupboard?" She would keep her husband and children in cupboards if she had her way: that would be her idea of the perfect home, everybody wrapped up with a piece of camphor in his or her own proper cupboard. I knew a woman once who was happy—for a woman. She lived in a house with twenty-nine cupboards: I think it must have been built by a woman. They were spacious cupboards, many of them, with doors in no way different from other doors. Visitors would wish each other good-night and disappear with their candles into cupboards, staggering out backwards the next moment, looking scared. One poor gentleman, this woman's husband told me, having to go downstairs again for something he had forgotten, and unable on his return to strike anything else but cupboards, lost heart and finished up the night in a cupboard. At breakfast-time guests would hurry down, and burst open cupboard doors with a cheery "Good-morning." When that woman was out, nobody in that house ever knew where anything was; and when she came home she herself only knew where it ought to have been. Yet once, when one of those twenty-nine cupboards had to be cleared out temporarily for repairs, she never smiled, her husband told me, for more than three weeks—not till the workmen were out of the house, and that cupboard in working order again. She said it was so confusing, having nowhere to put her things.

The average woman does not want a house, in the ordinary sense of the word. What she wants is something made by a genii. You have found, as you think, the ideal house. You show her the Adams fireplace in the drawing-room. You tap the wainscoting of the hall with your umbrella: "Oak," you impress upon her, "all oak." You draw her attention to the view: you tell her the local legend. By fixing her head against the window-pane she can see the tree on which the man was hanged. You dwell upon the sundial; you mention for a second time the Adams fireplace.

"It's all very nice," she answers, "but where are the children going to sleep?"

It is so disheartening.

If it isn't the children, it's the water. She wants water—wants to know where it comes from. You show her where it comes from.

"What, out of that nasty place!" she exclaims.

She is equally dissatisfied whether it be drawn from a well, or whether it be water that has fallen from heaven and been stored in tanks. She has no faith in Nature's water. A woman never believes that water can be good that does not come from a water-works. Her idea appears to be that the Company makes it fresh every morning from some old family recipe.

If you do succeed in reconciling her to the water, then she feels sure that the chimneys smoke; they look as if they smoked. Why—as you tell her—the chimneys are the best part of the house. You take her outside and make her look at them. They are genuine sixteenth-century chimneys, with carving on them. They couldn't smoke. They wouldn't do anything so inartistic. She says she only hopes you are right, and suggests cowls, if they do.

After that she wants to see the kitchen—where's the kitchen? You don't know where it is. You didn't bother about the kitchen. There must be a kitchen, of course. You proceed to search for the kitchen. When you find it she is worried because it is the opposite end of the house to the dining-room. You point out to her the advantage of being away from the smell of the cooking. At that she gets personal: tells you that you are the first to grumble when the dinner is cold; and in her madness accuses the whole male sex of being impractical. The mere sight of an empty house makes a woman fretful.

Of course the stove is wrong. The kitchen stove always is wrong. You promise she shall have a new one. Six months later she will want the old one back again: but it would be cruel to tell her this. The promise of that new stove comforts her. The woman never loses hope that one day it will come—the all-satisfying kitchen stove, the stove of her girlish dreams.

The question of the stove settled, you imagine you have silenced all opposition. At once she begins to talk about things that nobody but a woman or a sanitary inspector can talk about without blushing.

It calls for tact, getting a woman into a new house. She is nervous, suspicious.

"I am glad, my dear Dick," I answered; "that you have mentioned cupboards. It is with cupboards that I am hoping to lure your mother. The cupboards, from her point of view, will be the one bright spot; there are fourteen of them. I am trusting to cupboards to tide me over many things. I shall want you to come with me, Dick. Whenever your mother begins a sentence with: 'But now to be practical, dear,' I want you to murmur something about cupboards—not irritatingly as if it had been prearranged: have a little gumption."

"Will there be room for a tennis court?" demanded Dick.

"An excellent tennis court already exists," I informed him. "I have also purchased the adjoining paddock. We shall be able to keep our own cow. Maybe we'll breed horses."

"We might have a croquet lawn," suggested Robin.

"We might easily have a croquet lawn," I agreed. "On a full-sized lawn I believe Veronica might be taught to play. There are natures that demand space. On a full-sized lawn, protected by a stout iron border, less time might be wasted exploring the surrounding scenery for Veronica's lost ball."

"No chance of a golf links anywhere in the neighbourhood?" feared Dick.

"I am not so sure," I answered. "Barely a mile away there is a pretty piece of gorse land that appears to be no good to anyone. I daresay for a reasonable offer—"

"I say, when will this show be ready?" interrupted Dick.

"I propose beginning the alterations at once," I explained. "By luck there happens to be a gamekeeper's cottage vacant and within distance. The agent is going to get me the use of it for a year—a primitive little place, but charmingly situate on the edge of a wood. I shall furnish a couple of rooms; and for part of every week I shall make a point of being down there, superintending. I have always been considered good at superintending. My poor father used to say it was the only work I seemed to take an interest in. By being on the spot to hurry everybody on I hope to have the 'show,' as you term it, ready by the spring."

"I shall never marry," said Robin.

"Don't be so easily discouraged," advised Dick; "you are still young."

"I don't ever want to get married," continued Robin. "I should only quarrel with my husband, if I did. And Dick will never do anything—not with his head."

"Forgive me if I am dull," I pleaded, "but what is the connection between this house, your quarrels with your husband if you ever get one, and Dick's head?"

By way of explanation, Robin sprang to the ground, and before he could stop her had flung her arms around Dick's neck.

"We can't help it, Dick dear," she told him. "Clever parents always have duffing children. But we'll be of some use in the world after all, you and I."

The idea was that Dick, when he had finished failing in examinations, should go out to Canada and start a farm, taking Robin with him. They would breed cattle, and gallop over the prairies, and camp out in the primeval forest, and slide about on snow-shoes, and carry canoes on their backs, and shoot rapids, and stalk things—so far as I could gather, have a sort of everlasting Buffalo-Bill's show all to themselves. How and when the farm work was to get itself done was not at all clear. The Little Mother and myself were to end our days with them. We were to sit about in the sun for a time, and then pass peacefully away. Robin shed a few tears at this point, but regained her spirits, thinking of Veronica, who was to be lured out on a visit and married to some true-hearted yeoman: which is not at present Veronica's ambition. Veronica's conviction is that she would look well in a coronet: her own idea is something in the ducal line. Robina talked for about ten minutes. By the time she had done she had persuaded Dick that life in the backwoods of Canada had been his dream from infancy. She is that sort of girl.

I tried talking reason, but talking to Robin when she has got a notion in her head is like trying to fix a halter on a two-year-old colt. This tumble-down, six-roomed cottage was to be the saving of the family. An ecstatic look transfigured Robina's face even as she spoke of it. You might have fancied it a shrine. Robina would do the cooking. Robina would rise early and milk the cow, and gather the morning egg. We would lead the simple life, learn to fend for ourselves. It would be so good for Veronica. The higher education could wait; let the higher ideals have a chance. Veronica would make the beds, dust the rooms. In the evening Veronica, her little basket by her side, would sit and sew while I talked, telling them things, and Robina moved softly to and fro about her work, the household fairy. The Little Mother, whenever strong enough, would come to us. We would hover round her, tending her with loving hands. The English farmer must know something, in spite of all that is said. Dick could arrange for lessons in practical farming. She did not say it crudely; but hinted that, surrounded by example, even I might come to take an interest in honest labour, might end by learning to do something useful.

Robina talked, I should say, for a quarter of an hour. By the time she had done, it appeared to me rather a beautiful idea. Dick's vacation had just commenced. For the next three months there would be nothing else for him to do but—to employ his own expressive phrase—"rot round." In any event, it would be keeping him out of mischief. Veronica's governess was leaving. Veronica's governess generally does leave at the end of about a year. I think sometimes of advertising for a lady without a conscience. At the end of a year, they explain to me that their conscience will not allow them to remain longer; they do not feel they are earning their salary. It is not that the child is not a dear child, it is not that she is stupid. Simply it is—as a German lady to whom Dick had been giving what he called finishing lessons in English, once put it—that she does not seem to be "taking any." Her mother's idea is that it is "sinking in." Perhaps if we allowed Veronica to lie fallow for awhile, something might show itself. Robina, speaking for herself, held that a period of quiet usefulness, away from the society of other silly girls and sillier boys, would result in her becoming a sensible woman. It is not often that Robina's yearnings take this direction: to thwart them, when they did, seemed wrong.

We had some difficulty with the Little Mother. That these three babies of hers will ever be men and women capable of running a six-roomed cottage appears to the Little Mother in the light of a fantastic dream. I explained to her that I should be there, at all events for two or three days in every week, to give an eye to things. Even that did not content her. She gave way eventually on Robina's solemn undertaking that she should be telegraphed for the first time Veronica coughed.

On Monday we packed a one-horse van with what we deemed essential. Dick and Robina rode their bicycles. Veronica, supported by assorted bedding, made herself comfortable upon the tailboard. I followed down by train on the Wednesday afternoon.

III

I t was the cow that woke me the first morning. I did not know it was our cow—not at the time. I didn't know we had a cow. I looked at my watch; it was half-past two. I thought maybe she would go to sleep again, but her idea was that the day had begun. I went to the window, the moon was at the full. She was standing by the gate, her head inside the garden; I took it her anxiety was lest we might miss any of it. Her neck was stretched out straight, her eyes towards the sky; which gave to her the appearance of a long-eared alligator. I have never had much to do with cows. I don't know how you talk to them. I told her to "be quiet," and to "lie down"; and made pretence to throw a boot at her. It seemed to cheer her, having an audience; she added half a dozen extra notes. I never knew before a cow had so much in her. There is a thing one sometimes meets with in the suburbs—or one used to; I do not know whether it is still extant, but when I was a boy it was quite common. It has a hurdy-gurdy fixed to its waist and a drum strapped on behind, a row of pipes hanging from its face, and bells and clappers from most of its other joints. It plays them all at once, and smiles. This cow reminded me of it—with organ effects added. She didn't smile; there was that to be said in her favour.

I hoped that if I made believe to be asleep she would get discouraged. So I closed the window ostentatiously, and went back to bed. But it only had the effect of putting her on her mettle. "He did not care for that last," I imagined her saying to herself, "I wasn't at my best. There wasn't feeling enough in it." She kept it up for about half an hour, and then the gate against which, I suppose, she had been leaning, gave way with a crash. That frightened her, and I heard her gallop off across the field. I was on the point of dozing off again when a pair of pigeons settled on the window-sill and began to coo. It is a pretty sound when you are in the mood for it. I wrote a poem once—a simple thing, but instinct with longing—while sitting under a tree and listening to the cooing of a pigeon. But that was in the afternoon. My only longing now was for a gun. Three times I got out of bed and "shoo'd" them away. The third time I remained by the window till I had got it firmly into their heads that I really did not want them. My behaviour on the former two occasions they had evidently judged to be mere playfulness. I had just got back to bed again when an owl began to screech. That is another sound I used to think attractive—so weird, so mysterious. It is Swinburne, I think, who says that you never get the desired one and the time and the place all right together. If the beloved one is with you, it is the wrong place or at the wrong time; and if the time and the place happen to be right, then it is the party that is wrong. The owl was all right: I like owls. The place was all right. He had struck the wrong time, that was all. Eleven o'clock at night, when you can't see him, and naturally feel that you want to, is the proper time for an owl. Perched on the roof of a cow-shed in the early dawn he looks silly. He clung there, flapping his wings and screeching at the top of his voice. What it was he wanted I am sure I don't know; and anyhow it didn't seem the way to get it. He came to this conclusion himself at the end of twenty minutes, and shut himself up and went home. I thought I was going to have at last some peace, when a corncrake—a creature upon whom Nature has bestowed a song like to the tearing of calico-sheets mingled with the sharpening of saws—settled somewhere in the garden and set to work to praise its Maker according to its lights. I have a friend, a poet, who lives just off the Strand, and spends his evenings at the Garrick Club. He writes occasional verse for the evening papers, and talks about the "silent country, drowsy with the weight of languors." One of these times I'll lure him down for a Saturday to Monday and let him find out what the country really is—let him hear it. He is becoming too much of a dreamer: it will do him good, wake him up a bit. The corncrake after awhile stopped quite suddenly with a jerk, and for quite five minutes there was silence.

"If this continues for another five," I said to myself, "I'll be asleep." I felt it coming over me. I had hardly murmured the words when the cow turned up again. I should say she had been somewhere and had had a drink. She was in better voice than ever.

It occurred to me that this would be an opportunity to make a few notes on the sunrise. The literary man is looked to for occasional description of the sunrise. The earnest reader who has heard about this sunrise thirsts for full particulars. Myself, for purposes of observation, I have generally chosen December or the early part of January. But one never knows. Maybe one of these days I'll want a summer sunrise, with birds and dew-besprinkled flowers: it goes well with the rustic heroine, the miller's daughter, or the girl who brings up chickens and has dreams. I met a brother author once at seven o'clock in the morning in Kensington Gardens. He looked half asleep and so disagreeable that I hesitated for awhile to speak to him: he is a man that as a rule breakfasts at eleven. But I summoned my courage and accosted him.

"This is early for you," I said.

"It's early for anyone but a born fool," he answered.

"What's the matter?" I asked. "Can't you sleep?"

"Can't I sleep?" he retorted indignantly. "Why, I daren't sit down upon a seat, I daren't lean up against a tree. If I did I'd be asleep in half a second."

"What's the idea?" I persisted. "Been reading Smiles's 'Self Help and the Secret of Success'? Don't be absurd," I advised him. "You'll be going to Sunday school next and keeping a diary. You have left it too late: we don't reform at forty. Go home and go to bed." I could see he was doing himself no good.

"I'm going to bed," he answered, "I'm going to bed for a month when I've finished this confounded novel that I'm on. Take my advice," he said—he laid his hand upon my shoulder—"Never choose a colonial girl for your heroine. At our age it is simple madness."

"She's a fine girl," he continued, "and good. Has a heart of gold. She's wearing me to a shadow. I wanted something fresh and unconventional. I didn't grasp what it was going to do. She's the girl that gets up early in the morning and rides bare-back—the horse, I mean, of course; don't be so silly. Over in New South Wales it didn't matter. I threw in the usual local colour—the eucalyptus-tree and the kangaroo—and let her ride. It is now that she is over here in London that I wish I had never thought of her. She gets up at five and wanders about the silent city. That means, of course, that I have to get up at five in order to record her impressions. I have walked six miles this morning. First to St. Paul's Cathedral; she likes it when there's nobody about. You'd think it wasn't big enough for her to see if anybody else was in the street. She thinks of it as of a mother watching over her sleeping children; she's full of all that sort of thing. And from there to Westminster Bridge. She sits on the parapet and reads Wordsworth, till the policeman turns her off. This is another of her favourite spots." He indicated with a look of concentrated disgust the avenue where we were standing. "This is where she likes to finish up. She comes here to listen to a blackbird."

"Well, you are through with it now," I said to console him. "You've done it; and it's over."

"Through with it!" he laughed bitterly. "I'm just beginning it. There's the entire East End to be done yet: she's got to meet a fellow there as

JEROME K. JEROME

big a crank as herself. And walking isn't the worst. She's going to have a horse; you can guess what that means.—Hyde Park will be no good to her. She'll find out Richmond and Ham Common. I've got to describe the scenery and the mad joy of the thing."

"Can't you imagine it?" I suggested.

"I'm going to imagine all the enjoyable part of it," he answered. "I must have a groundwork to go upon. She's got to have feelings come to her upon this horse. You can't enter into a rider's feelings when you've almost forgotten which side of the horse you get up."

I walked with him to the Serpentine. I had been wondering how it was he had grown stout so suddenly. He had a bath towel round him underneath his coat.

"It'll give me my death of cold, I know it will," he chattered while unlacing his boots.

"Can't you leave it till the summer-time," I suggested, "and take her to Ostend?"

"It wouldn't be unconventional," he growled. "She wouldn't take an interest in it."

"But do they allow ladies to bathe in the Serpentine?" I persisted.

"It won't be the Serpentine," he explained. "It's going to be the Thames at Greenwich. But it must be the same sort of feeling. She's got to tell them all about it during a lunch in Queen's Gate, and shock them all. That's all she does it for, in my opinion."

He emerged a mottled blue. I helped him into his clothes, and he was fortunate enough to find an early cab. The book appeared at Christmas. The critics agreed that the heroine was a delightful creation. Some of them said they would like to have known her.

Remembering my poor friend, it occurred to me that by going out now and making a few notes about the morning, I might be saving myself trouble later on. I slipped on a few things—nothing elaborate—put a notebook in my pocket, opened the door and went down.

Perhaps it would be more correct to say "opened the door and was down." It was my own fault, I admit. We had talked this thing over before going to bed, and I myself had impressed upon Veronica the need for caution. The architect of the country cottage does not waste space. He dispenses with landings; the bedroom door opens on to the top stair. It does not do to walk out of your bedroom, for the reason there is nothing outside to walk on. I had said to Veronica, pointing out this fact to her:

"Now don't, in the morning, come bursting out of the room in your usual volcanic style, because if you do there will be trouble. As you perceive, there is no landing. The stairs commence at once; they are steep, and they lead down to a brick floor. Open the door quietly, look where you are going, and step carefully."

Dick had added his advice to mine. "I did that myself the first morning," Dick had said. "I stepped straight out of the bedroom into the kitchen; and I can tell you, it hurts. You be careful, young 'un. This cottage doesn't lend itself to dash."

Robina had fallen down with a tray in her hand. She said that never should she forget the horror of that moment, when, sitting on the kitchen floor, she had cried to Dick—her own voice sounding to her as if it came from somewhere quite far off: "Is it broken? Tell me the truth. Is it broken anywhere?" and Dick had replied: "Broken! why, it's smashed to atoms. What did you expect?" Robina had asked the question with reference to her head, while Dick had thought she was alluding to the teapot. In that moment, had said Robina, her whole life had passed before her. She let Veronica feel the bump.

Veronica was disappointed with the bump, having expected something bigger, but had promised to be careful. We had all agreed that if in spite of our warnings she forgot, and came blundering down in the morning, it would serve her right. It was thinking of all this that, as I lay upon the floor, made me feel angry with everybody. I hate people who can sleep through noises that wake me up. Why was I the only person in the house to be disturbed? Dick's room was round the corner; there was some excuse for him. But Robina and Veronica's window looked straight down upon the cow. If Robina and Veronica were not a couple of logs, the cow would have aroused them. We should have discussed the matter with the door ajar. Robina would have said, "Whatever you do, be careful of the stairs, Pa," and I should have remembered. The modern child appears to me to have no feeling for its parent.

I picked myself up and started for the door. The cow continued bellowing steadily. My whole anxiety was to get to her quickly and to hit her. But the door took more finding than I could have believed possible. The shutters were closed and the whole place was in pitch darkness. The idea had been to furnish this cottage only with things that were absolutely necessary, but the room appeared to me to be overcrowded. There was a milking-stool, which is a thing made purposely heavy so that it may not be easily upset. If I tumbled over it once I tumbled over it a dozen times. I got hold of it at last and carried it about with me. I thought I would use it to hit the cow—that is, when I had found the front-door. I knew it led out of the parlour, but could not recollect its exact position. I argued that if I kept along the wall I should be bound to come to it. I found the wall, and set off full of hope. I suppose the explanation was that, without knowing it, I must have started with the door, not the front-door, the other door, leading into the kitchen. I crept along, carefully feeling my way, and struck quite new things altogether—things I had no recollection of and that hit me in fresh places. I climbed over what I presumed to be a beer-barrel and landed among bottles; there were dozens upon dozens of them. To get away from these bottles I had to leave the wall; but I found it again, as I thought, and I felt along it for another half a dozen yards or so and then came again upon bottles: the room appeared to be paved with bottles. A little farther on I rolled over another beer-barrel: as a matter of fact it was the same beer-barrel, but I did not know this. At the time it seemed to me that Robina had made up her mind to run a public-house. I found the milking-stool again and started afresh, and before I had gone a dozen steps was in among bottles again. Later on, in the broad daylight, it was easy enough to understand what had happened. I had been carefully feeling my way round and round a screen. I got so sick of these bottles and so tired of rolling over these everlasting beer-barrels, that I abandoned the wall and plunged boldly into space.

I had barely started, when, looking up, I saw the sky above me: a star was twinkling just above my head. Had I been wide awake, and had the cow stopped bellowing for just one minute, I should have guessed that somehow or another I had got into a chimney. But as things were, the wonder and the mystery of it all appalled me. "Alice's Adventures in Wonderland" would have appeared to me, at that moment, in the nature of a guide to travellers. Had a rocking-horse or a lobster suddenly appeared to me I should have sat and talked to it; and if it had not answered me I should have thought it sulky and been hurt. I took a step forward and the star disappeared, just as if somebody had blown it out. I was not surprised in the least. I was expecting anything to happen.

I found a door and it opened quite easily. A wood was in front of me. I couldn't see any cow anywhere, but I still heard her. It all seemed quite natural. I would wander into the wood; most likely I should meet her there, and she would be smoking a pipe. In all probability she would know some poetry.

With the fresh air my senses gradually came back to me, and I began to understand why it was I could not see the cow. The reason was that the house was between us. By some mysterious process I had been discharged into the back garden. I still had the milking-stool in my hand, but the cow no longer troubled me. Let her see if she could wake Veronica by merely bellowing outside the door; it was more than I had ever been able to do.

I sat down on the stool and opened my note-book. I headed the page: "Sunrise in July: observations and emotions," and I wrote down at once, lest I should forget it, that towards three o'clock a faint light is discernible, and added that this light gets stronger as the time goes on.

It sounded footling even to myself, but I had been reading a novel of the realistic school that had been greatly praised for its actuality. There is a demand in some quarters for this class of observation. I likewise made a note that the pigeon and the corncrake appear to be among the earliest of Nature's children to welcome the coming day; and added that the screech-owl may be heard, perhaps at its best, by anyone caring to rise for the purpose, some quarter of an hour before the dawn. That was all I could think of just then. As regards emotions, I did not seem to have any.

I lit a pipe and waited for the sun. The sky in front of me was tinged with a faint pink. Every moment it flushed a deeper red. I maintain that anyone, not an expert, would have said that was the portion of the horizon on which to keep one's eye. I kept my eye upon it, but no sun appeared. I lit another pipe. The sky in front of me was now a blaze of glory. I scribbled a few lines, likening the scattered clouds to brides blushing at the approach of the bridegroom. That would have been all right if later on they hadn't begun to turn green: it seemed the wrong colour for a bride. Later on still they went yellow, and that spoilt the simile past hope. One cannot wax poetical about a bride who at the approach of the bridegroom turns first green and then yellow: you can only feel sorry for her. I waited some more. The sky in front of me grew paler every moment. I began to fear that something had happened to that sun. If I hadn't known so much astronomy I should have said that he had changed his mind and had gone back again. I rose with the idea of seeing into things. He had been up apparently for hours: he had got up at the back of me. It seemed to be nobody's fault. I put my pipe into my pocket and strolled round to the front. The cow was still there; she was pleased to see me, and started bellowing again.

I heard a sound of whistling. It proceeded from a farmer's boy. I hailed him, and he climbed a gate and came to me across the field. He was a cheerful youth. He nodded to the cow and hoped she had had a good night: he pronounced it "nihet."

"You know the cow?" I said.

"Well," he explained, "we don't precisely move in the sime set. Sort o' business relytionship more like—if you understand me?"

Something about this boy was worrying me. He did not seem like a real farmer's boy. But then nothing seemed quite real this morning. My feeling was to let things go.

"Whose cow is it?" I asked.

He stared at me.

"I want to know to whom it belongs," I said. "I want to restore it to him."

"Excuse me," said the boy, "but where do you live?"

He was making me cross. "Where do I live?" I retorted. "Why, in this cottage. You don't think I've got up early and come from a distance to listen to this cow? Don't talk so much. Do you know whose cow it is, or don't you?"

"It's your cow," said the boy.

It was my turn to stare.

"But I haven't got a cow," I told him.

"Yus you have," he persisted; "you've got that cow."

She had stopped bellowing for a moment. She was not the cow I felt I could ever take a pride in. At some time or another, quite recently, she must have sat down in some mud.

"How did I get her?" I demanded.

"The young lydy," explained the boy, "she came rahnd to our plice on Tuesday—"

I began to see light. "An excitable young lady—talks very fast— never waits for the answer?"

"With jolly fine eyes," added the boy approvingly.

"And she ordered a cow?"

"Didn't seem to 'ave strength enough to live another dy withaht it."

"Any stipulation made concerning the price of the cow?"

"Any what?"

"The young lady with the eyes—did she think to ask the price of the cow?"

"No sordid details was entered into, so far as I could 'ear," replied the boy.

They would not have been—by Robina.

"Any hint let fall as to what the cow was wanted for?"

"The lydy gives us to understand," said the boy, "that fresh milk was 'er idea."

That surprised me: that was thoughtful of Robina. "And this is the cow?"

"I towed her rahnd last night. I didn't knock at the door and tell yer abaht 'er, cos, to be quite frank with yer, there wasn't anybody in."

"What is she bellowing for?" I asked.

"Well," said the boy, "it's only a theory, o' course, but I should sy, from the look of 'er, that she wanted to be milked."

"But it started bellowing at half-past two," I argued. "It doesn't expect to be milked at half-past two, does it?"

"Meself," said the boy, "I've given up looking for sense in cows."

In some unaccountable way this boy was hypnotising me. Everything had suddenly become out of place.

The cow had suddenly become absurd: she ought to have been a milk-can. The wood struck me as neglected: there ought to have been notice-boards about, "Keep off the Grass," "Smoking Strictly Prohibited": there wasn't a seat to be seen. The cottage had surely got itself there by accident: where was the street? The birds were all out of their cages; everything was upside down.

"Are you a real farmer's boy?" I asked him.

"O' course I am," he answered. "What do yer tike me for—a hartist in disguise?"

It came to me. "What is your name?"

"'Enery—'Enery 'Opkins."

"Where were you born?"

"Camden Tahn."

Here was a nice beginning to a rural life! What place could be the country while this boy Hopkins was about? He would have given to the Garden of Eden the atmosphere of an outlying suburb.

"Do you want to earn an occasional shilling?" I put it to him.

"I'd rather it come reggler," said Hopkins. "Better for me kerrickter."

"You drop that Cockney accent and learn Berkshire, and I'll give you half a sovereign when you can talk it," I promised him. "Don't, for instance, say 'ain't,'" I explained to him. "Say 'bain't.' Don't say 'The young lydy, she came rahnd to our plice;' say 'The missy, 'er coomed down; 'er coomed, and 'er ses to the maister, 'er ses. . .' That's the sort of thing I want to surround myself with here. When you informed me that the cow was mine, you should have said: 'Whoi, 'er be your cow, surelie 'er be.'"

"Sure it's Berkshire?" demanded Hopkins. "You're confident about it?" There is a type that is by nature suspicious.

"It may not be Berkshire pure and undefiled," I admitted. "It is what in literature we term 'dialect.' It does for most places outside the twelve-mile radius. The object is to convey a feeling of rustic simplicity. Anyhow, it isn't Camden Town."

I started him with a shilling then and there to encourage him. He promised to come round in the evening for one or two books, written by friends of mine, that I reckoned would be of help to him; and I returned to the cottage and set to work to rouse Robina. Her tone was apologetic. She had got the notion into her head that I had been calling her for quite a long time. I explained that this was not the case.

"How funny!" she answered. "I said to Veronica more than an hour ago: 'I'm sure that's Pa calling us.' I suppose I must have been dreaming."

"Well, don't dream any more," I suggested. "Come down and see to this confounded cow of yours."

"Oh," said Veronica, "has it come?"

"It has come," I told her. "As a matter of fact, it has been here some time. It ought to have been milked four hours ago, according to its own idea."

Robina said she would be down in a minute.

She was down in twenty-five, which was sooner than I had expected. She brought Veronica with her. She said she would have been down sooner if she had not waited for Veronica. It appeared that this was just precisely what Veronica had been telling her. I was feeling irritable. I had been up half a day, and hadn't had my breakfast.

"Don't stand there arguing," I told them. "For goodness' sake let's get to work and milk this cow. We shall have the poor creature dying on our hands if we're not careful."

Robina was wandering round the room.

"You haven't come across a milking-stool anywhere, have you, Pa?" asked Robina.

"I have come across your milking-stool, I estimate, some thirteen times," I told her. I fetched it from where I had left it, and gave it to her;

and we filed out in procession; Veronica with a galvanised iron bucket bringing up the rear.

The problem that was forcing itself upon my mind was: did Robina know how to milk a cow? Robina, I argued, the idea once in her mind, would immediately have ordered a cow, clamouring for it—as Hopkins had picturesquely expressed it—as though she had not strength to live another day without a cow. Her next proceeding would have been to buy a milking-stool. It was a tasteful milking-stool, this one she had selected, ornamented with the rough drawing of a cow in poker work: a little too solid for my taste, but one that I should say would wear well. The pail she had not as yet had time to see about. This galvanised bucket we were using was, I took it, a temporary makeshift. When Robina had leisure she would go into the town and purchase something at an art stores. That, to complete the scheme, she would have done well to have taken a few practical lessons in milking would come to her, as an inspiration, with the arrival of the cow. I noticed that Robina's steps as we approached the cow were less elastic. Just outside the cow Robina halted.

"I suppose," said Robina, "there's only one way of milking a cow?"

"There may be fancy ways," I answered, "necessary to you if later on you think of entering a competition. This morning, seeing we are late, I shouldn't worry too much about style. If I were you, this morning I should adopt the ordinary unimaginative method, and aim only at results."

Robina sat down and placed her bucket underneath the cow.

"I suppose," said Robina, "it doesn't matter which—which one I begin with?"

It was perfectly plain she hadn't the least notion how to milk a cow. I told her so, adding comments. Now and then a little fatherly talk does good. As a rule I have to work myself up for these occasions. This morning I was feeling fairly fit: things had conspired to this end. I put before Robina the aims and privileges of the household fairy as they appeared, not to her, but to me. I also confided to Veronica the result of many weeks' reflections concerning her and her behaviour. I also told them both what I thought about Dick. I do this sort of thing once every six months: it has an excellent effect for about three days.

Robina wiped away her tears, and seized the first one that came to her hand. The cow, without saying a word, kicked over the empty bucket, and walked away, disgust expressed in every hair of her body.

Robina, crying quietly, followed her. By patting her on her neck, and letting her wipe her nose upon my coat—which seemed to comfort her—I persuaded her to keep still while Robina worked for ten minutes at high pressure. The result was about a glassful and a half, the cow's capacity, to all appearance, being by this time some five or six gallons.

Robina broke down, and acknowledged she had been a wicked girl. If the cow died, so she said, she should never forgive herself. Veronica at this burst into tears also; and the cow, whether moved afresh by her own troubles or by theirs, commenced again to bellow. I was fortunately able to find an elderly labourer smoking a pipe and eating bacon underneath a tree; and with him I bargained that for a shilling a day he should milk the cow till further notice.

We left him busy, and returned to the cottage. Dick met us at the door with a cheery "Good morning." He wanted to know if we had heard the storm. He also wanted to know when breakfast would be ready. Robina thought that happy event would be shortly after he had boiled the kettle and made the tea and fried the bacon, while Veronica was laying the table.

"But I thought—"

Robina said that if he dared to mention the word "household-fairy" she would box his ears, and go straight up to bed, and leave everybody to do everything. She said she meant it.

Dick has one virtue: it is philosophy. "Come on, young 'un," said Dick to Veronica. "Trouble is good for us all."

"Some of us," said Veronica, "it makes bitter."

We sat down to breakfast at eight-thirty.

IV

O ur architect arrived on Friday afternoon, or rather, his assistant.
I felt from the first I was going to like him. He is shy, and that,
of course, makes him appear awkward. But, as I explained to Robina, it
is the shy young men who, generally speaking, turn out best: few men
could have been more painfully shy up to twenty-five than myself.

Robina said that was different: in the case of an author it did not
matter. Robina's attitude towards the literary profession would not
annoy me so much were it not typical. To be a literary man is, in Robina's
opinion, to be a licensed idiot. It was only a week or two ago that I
overheard from my study window a conversation between Veronica
and Robina upon this very point. Veronica's eye had caught something
lying on the grass. I could not myself see what it was, in consequence
of an intervening laurel bush. Veronica stooped down and examined
it with care. The next instant, uttering a piercing whoop, she leapt
into the air; then, clapping her hands, began to dance. Her face was
radiant with a holy joy. Robina, passing near, stopped and demanded
explanation.

"Pa's tennis racket!" shouted Veronica—Veronica never sees the use
of talking in an ordinary tone of voice when shouting will do just as well.
She continued clapping her hands and taking little bounds into the air.

"Well, what are you going on like that for?" asked Robina. "It hasn't
bit you, has it?"

"It's been out all night in the wet," shouted Veronica. "He forgot to
bring it in."

"You wicked child!" said Robina severely. "It's nothing to be pleased
about."

"Yes, it is," explained Veronica. "I thought at first it was mine. Oh,
wouldn't there have been a talk about it, if it had been! Oh my! wouldn't
there have been a row!" She settled down to a steady rhythmic dance,
suggestive of a Greek chorus expressing satisfaction with the gods.

Robina seized her by the shoulders and shook her back into herself.
"If it had been yours," said Robina, "you would deserve to have been
sent to bed."

"Well, then, why don't he go to bed?" argued Veronica.

Robina took her by the arm and walked her up and down just
underneath my window. I listened, because the conversation interested me.

"Pa, as I am always explaining to you," said Robina, "is a literary man. He cannot help forgetting things."

"Well, I can't help forgetting things," insisted Veronica.

"You find it hard," explained Robina kindly; "but if you keep on trying you will succeed. You will get more thoughtful. I used to be forgetful and do foolish things once, when I was a little girl."

"Good thing for us if we was all literary," suggested Veronica.

"If we 'were' all literary," Robina corrected her. "But you see we are not. You and I and Dick, we are just ordinary mortals. We must try and think, and be sensible. In the same way, when Pa gets excited and raves—I mean, seems to rave—it's the literary temperament. He can't help it."

"Can't you help doing anything when you are literary?" asked Veronica.

"There's a good deal you can't help," answered Robina. "It isn't fair to judge them by the ordinary standard."

They drifted towards the kitchen garden—it was the time of strawberries—and the remainder of the talk I lost. I noticed that for some days afterwards Veronica displayed a tendency to shutting herself up in the schoolroom with a copybook, and that lead pencils had a way of disappearing from my desk. One in particular that had suited me I determined if possible to recover. A subtle instinct guided me to Veronica's sanctum. I found her thoughtfully sucking it. She explained to me that she was writing a little play.

"You get things from your father, don't you?" she enquired of me.

"You do," I admitted; "but you ought not to take them without asking. I am always telling you of it. That pencil is the only one I can write with."

"I didn't mean the pencil," explained Veronica. "I was wondering if I had got your literary temper."

It is puzzling, when you come to think of it, this estimate accorded by the general public to the *littérateur*. It stands to reason that the man who writes books, explaining everything and putting everybody right, must be himself an exceptionally clever man; else how could he do it! The thing is pure logic. Yet to listen to Robina and her like you might think we had not sense enough to run ourselves, as the saying is—let alone running the universe. If I would let her, Robina would sit and give me information by the hour.

"The ordinary girl. . ." Robina will begin, with the air of a University Extension Lecturer.

It is so exasperating. As if I did not know all there is to be known about girls! Why, it is my business. I point this out to Robina.

"Yes, I know," Robina will answer sweetly. "But I was meaning the real girl."

It would make not the slightest difference were I even quite a high-class literary man—Robina thinks I am: she is a dear child. Were I Shakespeare himself, and could I in consequence say to her: "Methinks, child, the creator of Ophelia and Juliet, and Rosamund and Beatrice, must surely know something about girls," Robina would still make answer:

"Of course, Pa dear. Everybody knows how clever you are. But I was thinking for the moment of real girls."

I wonder to myself sometimes, Is literature to the general reader ever anything more than a fairy-tale? We write with our heart's blood, as we put it. We ask our conscience, Is it right thus to lay bare the secrets of our souls? The general reader does not grasp that we are writing with our heart's blood: to him it is just ink. He does not believe we are laying bare the secrets of our souls: he takes it we are just pretending. "Once upon a time there lived a girl named Angelina who loved a party by the name of Edwin." He imagines—he, the general reader—when we tell him all the wonderful thoughts that were inside Angelina, that it was we who put them there. He does not know, he will not try to understand, that Angelina is in reality more real than is Miss Jones, who rides up every morning in the 'bus with him, and has a pretty knack of rendering conversation about the weather novel and suggestive. As a boy I won some popularity among my schoolmates as a teller of stories. One afternoon, to a small collection with whom I was homing across Regent's Park, I told the story of a beautiful Princess. But she was not the ordinary Princess. She would not behave as a Princess should. I could not help it. The others heard only my voice, but I was listening to the wind. She thought she loved the Prince—until he had wounded the Dragon unto death and had carried her away into the wood. Then, while the Prince lay sleeping, she heard the Dragon calling to her in its pain, and crept back to where it lay bleeding, and put her arms about its scaly neck and kissed it; and that healed it. I was hoping myself that at this point it would turn into a prince itself, but it didn't; it just remained a dragon—so the wind said. Yet the Princess loved it: it wasn't half a bad dragon, when you knew it. I could not tell them what became of the Prince: the wind didn't seem to care a hang about the Prince.

Myself, I liked the story, but Hocker, who was a Fifth Form boy, voicing our little public, said it was rot, so far, and that I had got to hurry up and finish things rightly.

"But that is all," I told them.

"No, it isn't," said Hocker. "She's got to marry the Prince in the end. He'll have to kill the Dragon again; and mind he does it properly this time. Whoever heard of a Princess leaving a Prince for a Dragon!"

"But she wasn't the ordinary sort of Princess," I argued.

"Then she's got to be," criticised Hocker. "Don't you give yourself so many airs. You make her marry the Prince, and be slippy about it. I've got to catch the four-fifteen from Chalk Farm station."

"But she didn't," I persisted obstinately. "She married the Dragon and lived happy ever afterwards."

Hocker adopted sterner measures. He seized my arm and twisted it behind me.

"She married who?" demanded Hocker: grammar was not Hocker's strong point.

"The Dragon," I growled.

"She married who?" repeated Hocker.

"The Dragon," I whined.

"She married who?" for the third time urged Hocker.

Hocker was strong, and the tears were forcing themselves into my eyes in spite of me. So the Princess in return for healing the Dragon made it promise to reform. It went back with her to the Prince, and made itself generally useful to both of them for the rest of the tour. And the Prince took the Princess home with him and married her; and the Dragon died and was buried. The others liked the story better, but I hated it; and the wind sighed and died away.

The little crowd becomes the reading public, and Hocker grows into an editor; he twists my arm in other ways. Some are brave, so the crowd kicks them and scurries off to catch the four-fifteen. But most of us, I fear, are slaves to Hocker. Then, after awhile, the wind grows sulky and will not tell us stories any more, and we have to make them up out of our own heads. Perhaps it is just as well. What were doors and windows made for but to keep out the wind.

He is a dangerous fellow, this wandering Wind; he leads me astray. I was talking about our architect.

He made a bad start, so far as Robina was concerned, by coming in at the back-door. Robina, in a big apron, was washing up. He apologised for having blundered into the kitchen, and offered to go out again and work round to the front. Robina replied, with unnecessary severity as I thought, that an architect, if anyone, might have known the difference between the right side of a house and the wrong; but presumed that youth and inexperience could always be pleaded as excuse for stupidity. I cannot myself see why Robina should have been so much annoyed. Labour, as Robina had been explaining to Veronica only a few hours before, exalts a woman. In olden days, ladies—the highest in the land—were proud, not ashamed, of their ability to perform domestic duties. This, later on, I pointed out to Robina. Her answer was that in olden days you didn't have chits of boys going about, calling themselves architects, and opening back-doors without knocking; or if they did knock, knocking so that nobody on earth could hear them.

Robina wiped her hands on the towel behind the door, and brought him into the front-room, where she announced him, coldly, as "The young man from the architect's office." He explained—but quite modestly—that he was not exactly Messrs. Spreight's young man, but an architect himself, a junior member of the firm. To make it clear he produced his card, which was that of Mr. Archibald T. Bute, F.R.I.B.A. Practically speaking, all this was unnecessary. Through the open door I had, of course, heard every word; and old Spreight had told me of his intention to send me one of his most promising assistants, who would be able to devote himself entirely to my work. I put matters right by introducing him formally to Robina. They bowed to one another rather stiffly. Robina said that if he would excuse her she would return to her work; and he answered "Charmed," and also that he didn't mean it. As I have tried to get it into Robina's head, the young fellow was confused. He had meant—it was self-evident—that he was charmed at being introduced to her, not at her desire to return to the kitchen. But Robina appears to have taken a dislike to him.

I gave him a cigar, and we started for the house. It lies just a mile from this cottage, the other side of the wood. One excellent trait in him I soon discovered—he is intelligent without knowing everything.

I confess it to my shame, but the young man who knows everything has come to pall upon me. According to Emerson, this is a proof of my own intellectual feebleness. The strong man, intellectually, cultivates the society of his superiors. He wants to get on, he wants to learn things. If I loved knowledge as one should, I would have no one but young men about me. There was a friend of Dick's, a gentleman from Rugby. At one time he had hopes of me; I felt he had. But he was too impatient. He tried to bring me on too quickly. You must take into consideration natural capacity. After listening to him for an hour or two my mind would wander. I could not help it. The careless laughter of uninformed middle-aged gentlemen and ladies would creep to me from the croquet lawn or from the billiard-room. I longed to be among them. Sometimes I would battle with my lower nature. What did they know? What could they tell me? More often I would succumb. There were occasions when I used to get up and go away from him, quite suddenly.

I talked with young Bute during our walk about domestic architecture in general. He said he should describe the present tendency in domestic architecture as towards corners. The desire of the British public was to go into a corner and live. A lady for whose husband his firm had lately built a house in Surrey had propounded to him a problem in connection with this point. She agreed it was a charming house; no house in Surrey had more corners, and that was saying much. But she could not see how for the future she was going to bring up her children. She was a humanely minded lady. Hitherto she had punished them, when needful, by putting them in the corner; the shame of it had always exercised upon them a salutary effect. But in the new house corners are reckoned the prime parts of every room. It is the honoured guest who is sent into the corner. The father has a corner sacred to himself, with high up above his head a complicated cupboard, wherein with the help of a step-ladder, he may keep his pipes and his tobacco, and thus by slow degrees cure himself of the habit of smoking. The mother likewise has her corner, where stands her spinning-wheel, in case the idea comes to her to weave sheets and underclothing. It also has a book-shelf supporting thirteen volumes, arranged in a sloping position to look natural; the last one maintained at its angle of forty-five degrees by a ginger-jar in old blue Nankin. You are not supposed to touch them, because that would disarrange them. Besides which, fooling about, you might upset the ginger-jar. The consequence of all this is the corner is no longer disgraceful. The parent can no more say to the erring child:

"You wicked boy! Go into the cosy corner this very minute!"

In the house of the future the place of punishment will have to be the middle of the room. The angry mother will exclaim:

"Don't you answer me, you saucy minx! You go straight into the middle of the room, and don't you dare to come out of it till I tell you!"

The difficulty with the artistic house is finding the right people to put into it. In the picture the artistic room never has anybody in it. There is a strip of art embroidery upon the table, together with a bowl of roses. Upon the ancient high-backed settee lies an item of fancy work, unfinished—just as she left it. In the "study" an open book, face downwards, has been left on a chair. It is the last book he was reading—it has never been disturbed. A pipe of quaint design is cold upon the lintel of the lattice window. No one will ever smoke that pipe again: it must have been difficult to smoke at any time. The sight of the artistic room, as depicted in the furniture catalogue, always brings tears to my eyes. People once inhabited these rooms, read there those old volumes bound in vellum, smoked—or tried to smoke—these impracticable pipes; white hands, that someone maybe had loved to kiss, once fluttered among the folds of these unfinished antimacassars, or Berlin wool-work slippers, and went away, leaving the things about.

One takes it that the people who once occupied these artistic rooms are now all dead. This was their "Dining-Room." They sat on those artistic chairs. They could hardly have used the dinner service set out upon the Elizabethan dresser, because that would have left the dresser bare: one assumes they had an extra service for use, or else that they took their meals in the kitchen. The "Entrance Hall" is a singularly chaste apartment. There is no necessity for a door-mat: people with muddy boots, it is to be presumed, were sent round to the back. A riding-cloak, the relic apparently of a highwayman, hangs behind the door. It is the sort of cloak you would expect to find there—a decorative cloak. An umbrella or a waterproof cape would be fatal to the whole effect.

Now and again the illustrator of the artistic room will permit a young girl to come and sit there. But she has to be a very carefully selected girl. To begin with, she has got to look and dress as though she had been born at least three hundred years ago. She has got to have that sort of clothes, and she has got to have her hair done just that way.

She has got to look sad; a cheerful girl in the artistic room would jar one's artistic sense. One imagines the artist consulting with the proud possessor of the house.

"You haven't got such a thing as a miserable daughter, have you? Some fairly good-looking girl who has been crossed in love, or is misunderstood. Because if so, you might dress her up in something out of the local museum and send her along. A little thing like that gives verisimilitude to a design."

She must not touch anything. All she may do is to read a book—not really read it, that would suggest too much life and movement: she sits with the book in her lap and gazes into the fire, if it happens to be the dining-room: or out of the window if it happens to be a morning-room, and the architect wishes to call attention to the window-seat. Nothing of the male species, as far as I have been able to ascertain, has ever entered these rooms. I once thought I had found a man who had been allowed into his own "Smoking-Den," but on closer examination it turned out he was only a portrait.

Sometimes one is given "Vistas." Doors stand open, and you can see right away through "The Nook" into the garden. There is never a living soul about the place. The whole family has been sent out for a walk or locked up in the cellars. This strikes you as odd until you come to think the matter out. The modern man and woman is not artistic. I am not artistic—not what I call really artistic. I don't go well with Gobelin tapestry and warming-pans. I feel I don't. Robina is not artistic, not in that sense. I tried her once with a harpsichord I picked up cheap in Wardour Street, and a reproduction of a Roman stool. The thing was an utter failure. A cottage piano, with a photo-frame and a fern upon, it is what the soul cries out for in connection with Robina. Dick is not artistic. Dick does not go with peacocks' feathers and guitars. I can see Dick with a single peacock's feather at St. Giles's Fair, when the bulldogs are not looking; but the decorative panel of peacock's feathers is too much for him. I can imagine him with a banjo—but a guitar decorated with pink ribbons! To begin with he is not dressed for it. Unless a family be prepared to make themselves up as troubadours or cavaliers and to talk blank verse, I don't see how they can expect to be happy living in these fifteenth-century houses. The modern family— the old man in baggy trousers and a frock-coat he could not button if he tried to; the mother of figure distinctly Victorian; the boys in flannel suits and collars up to their ears; the girls in motor caps—are as incongruous in these mediæval dwellings as a party of Cook's tourists drinking bottled beer in the streets of Pompeii.

The designer of "The Artistic Home" is right in keeping to still life. In the artistic home—to paraphrase Dr. Watts—every prospect pleases and only man is inartistic. In the picture, the artistic bedroom, "in apple green, the bedstead of cherry-wood, with a touch of turkey-red throughout the draperies," is charming. It need hardly be said the bed is empty. Put a man or woman in that cherry-wood bed—I don't care how artistic they may think themselves—the charm would be gone. The really artistic party, one supposes, has a little room behind, where he sleeps and dresses himself. He peeps in at the door of this artistic bedroom, maybe occasionally enters to change the roses.

Imagine the artistic nursery five minutes after the real child had been let loose in it. I know a lady who once spent hundreds of pounds on an artistic nursery. She showed it to her friends with pride. The children were allowed in there on Sunday afternoons. I did an equally silly thing myself not long ago. Lured by a furniture catalogue, I started Robina in a boudoir. I gave it to her as a birthday-present. We have both regretted it ever since. Robina reckons she could have had a bicycle, a diamond bracelet, and a mandoline, and I should have saved money. I did the thing well. I told the furniture people I wanted it just as it stood in the picture: "Design for bedroom and boudoir combined, suitable for young girl, in teak, with sparrow blue hangings." We had everything: the antique fire arrangements that a vestal virgin might possibly have understood; the candlesticks, that were pictures in themselves, until we tried to put candles in them; the book-case and writing-desk combined, that wasn't big enough to write on, and out of which it was impossible to get a book until you had abandoned the idea of writing and had closed the cover; the enclosed washstand, that shut down and looked like an old bureau, with the inevitable bowl of flowers upon it that had to be taken off and put on the floor whenever you wanted to use the thing as a washstand; the toilet-table, with its cunning little glass, just big enough to see your nose in; the bedstead, hidden away behind the "thinking corner," where the girl couldn't get at it to make it. A prettier room you could not have imagined, till Robina started sleeping in it. I think she tried. Girl friends of hers, to whom she had bragged about it, would drop in and ask to be allowed to see it. Robina would say, "Wait a minute," and would run up and slam the door; and we would hear her for the next half-hour or so rushing round opening and shutting drawers and dragging things about. By the time it was a boudoir again she was exhausted and irritable. She wants now to give it up to Veronica, but Veronica objects to the position, which is between the bathroom and my study. Her idea is a room more removed, where she would be able to shut herself in and do her work, as she explains, without fear of interruption.

Young Bute told me that a friend of his, a well-to-do young fellow, who lived in Piccadilly, had had the whim to make his flat the reproduction of a Roman villa. There were of course no fires, the rooms were warmed by hot air from the kitchen. They had a cheerless aspect on a November afternoon, and nobody knew exactly where to sit. Light was obtained in the evening from Grecian lamps, which made it easy to understand why the ancient Athenians, as a rule, went to bed early. You dined sprawling on a couch. This was no doubt practicable when you took your plate into your hand and fed yourself with your fingers; but with a knife and fork the meal had all the advantages of a hot picnic. You did not feel luxurious or even wicked: you only felt nervous about your clothes. The thing lacked completeness. He could not expect his friends to come to him in Roman togas, and even his own man declined firmly to wear the costume of a Roman slave. The compromise was unsatisfactory, even from the purely pictorial point of view. You cannot be a Roman patrician of the time of Antoninus when you happen to live in Piccadilly at the opening of the twentieth century. All you can do is to make your friends uncomfortable and spoil their dinner for them. Young Bute said that, so far as he was concerned, he would always rather have spent the evening with his little nephews and nieces, playing at horses; it seemed to him a more sensible game.

Young Bute said that, speaking as an architect, he of course admired the ancient masterpieces of his art. He admired the Erechtheum at Athens; but Spurgeon's Tabernacle in the Old Kent Road built upon the same model would have irritated him. For a Grecian temple you wanted Grecian skies and Grecian girls. He said that, even as it was, Westminster Abbey in the season was an eyesore to him. The Dean and Choir in their white surplices passed muster, but the congregation in its black frock-coats and Paris hats gave him the same sense of incongruity as would a banquet of barefooted friars in the dining-hall of the Cannon Street Hotel.

It struck me there was sense in what he said. I decided not to mention my idea of carving 1553 above the front-door.

He said he could not understand this passion of the modern house-builder for playing at being a Crusader or a Canterbury Pilgrim. A retired Berlin boot-maker of his acquaintance had built himself a miniature Roman Castle near Heidelberg. They played billiards in the dungeon, and let off fireworks on the Kaiser's birthday from the roof of the watch-tower.

Another acquaintance of his, a draper at Holloway, had built himself a moated grange. The moat was supplied from the water-works under special arrangement, and all the electric lights were imitation candles. He had done the thing thoroughly. He had even designed a haunted chamber in blue, and a miniature chapel, which he used as a telephone closet. Young Bute had been invited down there for the shooting in the autumn. He said he could not be sure whether he was doing right or wrong, but his intention was to provide himself with a bow and arrows.

A change was coming over this young man. We had talked on other subjects and he had been shy and deferential. On this matter of bricks and mortar he spoke as one explaining things.

I ventured to say a few words in favour of the Tudor house. The Tudor house, he argued, was a fit and proper residence for the Tudor citizen—for the man whose wife rode behind him on a pack-saddle, who conducted his correspondence by the help of a moss-trooper. The Tudor fireplace was designed for folks to whom coal was unknown, and who left their smoking to their chimneys. A house that looked ridiculous with a motor-car before the door, where the electric bell jarred upon one's sense of fitness every time one heard it, was out of date, he maintained.

"For you, sir," he continued, "a twentieth-century writer, to build yourself a Tudor House would be as absurd as for Ben Jonson to have planned himself a Norman Castle with a torture-chamber underneath the wine-cellar, and the fireplace in the middle of the dining-hall. His fellow cronies of the Mermaid would have thought him stark, staring mad."

There was reason in what he was saying. I decided not to mention my idea of altering the chimneys and fixing up imitation gables, especially as young Bute seemed pleased with the house, which by this time we had reached.

"Now, that is a good house," said young Bute. "That is a house where a man in a frock-coat and trousers can sit down and not feel himself a stranger from another age. It was built for a man who wore a frock-coat and trousers—on weekdays, maybe, gaiters and a shooting-coat. You can enjoy a game of billiards in that house without the feeling that comes to you when playing tennis in the shadow of the Pyramids."

We entered, and I put before him my notions—such of them as I felt he would approve. We were some time about the business, and when we looked at our watches young Bute's last train to town had gone. There still remained much to talk about, and I suggested he should return with me to the cottage and take his luck. I could sleep with Dick and he could have my room. I told him about the cow, but he said he was a practised sleeper and would be delighted, if I could lend him a night-shirt, and if I thought Miss Robina would not be put out. I assured him that it would be a good thing for Robina; the unexpected guest would be a useful lesson to her in housekeeping. Besides, as I pointed out to him, it didn't really matter even if Robina were put out.

"Not to you, sir, perhaps," he answered, with a smile. "It is not with you that she will be indignant."

"That will be all right, my boy," I told him; "I take all responsibility."

"And I shall get all the blame," he laughed.

But, as I pointed out to him, it really didn't matter whom Robina blamed. We talked about women generally on our way back. I told him—impressing upon him there was no need for it to go farther—that I personally had come to the conclusion that the best way to deal with women was to treat them all as children. He agreed it might be a good method, but wanted to know what you did when they treated you as a child.

I know a most delightful couple: they have been married nearly twenty years, and both will assure you that an angry word has never passed between them. He calls her his "Little One," although she must be quite six inches taller than himself, and is never tired of patting her hand or pinching her ear. They asked her once in the drawing-room—so the Little Mother tells me—her recipe for domestic bliss. She said the mistake most women made was taking men too seriously.

"They are just overgrown children, that's all they are, poor dears," she laughed.

There are two kinds of love: there is the love that kneels and looks upward, and the love that looks down and pats. For durability I am prepared to back the latter.

The architect had died out of young Bute; he was again a shy young man during our walk back to the cottage. My hand was on the latch when he stayed me.

"Isn't this the back-door again, sir?" he enquired.

It was the back-door; I had not noticed it.

"Hadn't we better go round to the front, sir, don't you think?" he said.

"It doesn't matter—" I began.

But he had disappeared. So I followed him, and we entered by the front. Robina was standing by the table, peeling potatoes.

"I have brought Mr. Bute back with me," I explained. "He is going to stop the night."

Robina said: "If ever I go to live in a cottage again it will have one door." She took her potatoes with her and went upstairs.

"I do hope she isn't put out," said young Bute.

"Don't worry yourself," I comforted him. "Of course she isn't put out. Besides, I don't care if she is. She's got to get used to being put out; it's part of the lesson of life."

I took him upstairs, meaning to show him his bedroom and take my own things out of it. The doors of the two bedrooms were opposite one another. I made a mistake and opened the wrong door. Robina, still peeling potatoes, was sitting on the bed.

I explained we had made a mistake. Robina said it was of no consequence whatever, and, taking the potatoes with her, went downstairs again. Looking out of the window, I saw her making towards the wood. She was taking the potatoes with her.

"I do wish we hadn't opened the door of the wrong room," groaned young Bute.

"What a worrying chap you are!" I said to him. "Look at the thing from the humorous point of view. It's funny when you come to think of it. Wherever the poor girl goes, trying to peel her potatoes in peace and quietness, we burst in upon her. What we ought to do now is to take a walk in the wood. It is a pretty wood. We might say we had come to pick wild flowers."

But I could not persuade him. He said he had letters to write, and, if I would allow him, would remain in his room till dinner was ready.

Dick and Veronica came in a little later. Dick had been to see Mr. St. Leonard to arrange about lessons in farming. He said he thought I should like the old man, who wasn't a bit like a farmer. He had brought Veronica back in one of her good moods, she having met there and fallen in love with a donkey. Dick confided to me that, without committing himself, he had hinted to Veronica that if she would remain good for quite a long while I might be induced to buy it for her. It was a sturdy little animal, and could be made useful. Anyhow, it would give Veronica an object in life—something to strive for—which was just what she wanted. He is a thoughtful lad at times, is Dick.

The dinner was more successful than I had hoped for. Robina gave us melon as a *hors d'œuvre*, followed by sardines and a fowl, with potatoes and vegetable marrow. Her cooking surprised me. I had warned young Bute that it might be necessary to regard this dinner rather as a joke than as an evening meal, and was prepared myself to extract amusement from it rather than nourishment. My disappointment was agreeable. One can always imagine a comic dinner.

I dined once with a newly married couple who had just returned from their honeymoon. We ought to have sat down at eight o'clock; we sat down instead at half-past ten. The cook had started drinking in the morning; by seven o'clock she was speechless. The wife, giving up hope at a quarter to eight, had cooked the dinner herself. The other guests were sympathised with, but all I got was congratulation.

"He'll write something so funny about this dinner," they said.

You might have thought the cook had got drunk on purpose to oblige me. I have never been able to write anything funny about that dinner; it depresses me to this day, merely thinking of it.

We finished up with a cold trifle and some excellent coffee that Robina brewed over a lamp on the table while Dick and Veronica cleared away. It was one of the jolliest little dinners I have ever eaten; and, if Robina's figures are to be trusted, cost exactly six-and-fourpence for the five of us. There being no servants about, we talked freely and enjoyed ourselves. I began once at a dinner to tell a good story about a Scotchman, when my host silenced me with a look. He is a kindly man, and had heard the story before. He explained to me afterwards, over the walnuts, that his parlourmaid was Scotch and rather touchy. The talk fell into the discussion of Home Rule, and again our host silenced us. It seemed his butler was an Irishman and a violent Parnellite. Some people can talk as though servants were mere machines, but to me they are human beings, and their presence hampers me. I know my guests have not heard the story before, and from one's own flesh and blood one expects a certain amount of sacrifice. But I feel so sorry for the housemaid who is waiting; she must have heard it a dozen times. I really cannot inflict it upon her again.

After dinner we pushed the table into a corner, and Dick extracted a sort of waltz from Robina's mandoline. It is years since I danced; but Veronica said she would rather dance with me any day than with some of the "lumps" you were given to drag round by the dancing-mistress. I have half a mind to take it up again. After all, a man is only as old as he feels.

Young Bute, it turned out, was a capital dancer, and could even reverse, which in a room fourteen feet square is of advantage. Robina confided to me after he was gone that while he was dancing she could just tolerate him. I cannot myself see rhyme or reason in Robina's objection to him. He is not handsome, but he is good-looking, as boys go, and has a pleasant smile. Robina says it is his smile that maddens her. Dick agrees with me that there is sense in him; and Veronica, not given to loose praise, considers his performance of a Red Indian, both dead and alive, the finest piece of acting she has ever encountered. We wound up the evening with a little singing. The extent of Dick's repertoire surprised me; evidently he has not been so idle at Cambridge as it seemed. Young Bute has a baritone voice of some richness. We remembered at quarter-past eleven that Veronica ought to have gone to bed at eight. We were all of us surprised at the lateness of the hour.

"Why can't we always live in a cottage and do just as we like? I'm sure it's much jollier," Veronica put it to me as I kissed her good night.

"Because we are idiots, most of us, Veronica," I answered.

V

I started the next morning to call upon St. Leonard. Near to the house I encountered young Hopkins on a horse. He was waving a pitchfork over his head and reciting "The Charge of the Light Brigade." The horse looked amused. He told me I should find "the gov'nor" up by the stables. St. Leonard is not an "old man." Dick must have seen him in a bad light. I should describe him as about the prime of life, a little older than myself, but nothing to speak of. Dick was right, however, in saying he was not like a farmer. To begin with, "Hubert St. Leonard" does not sound like a farmer. One can imagine a man with a name like that writing a book about farming, having theories on this subject. But in the ordinary course of nature things would not grow for him. He does not look like a farmer. One cannot say precisely what it is, but there is that about a farmer that tells you he is a farmer. The farmer has a way of leaning over a gate. There are not many ways of leaning over a gate. I have tried all I could think of, but it was never quite the right way. It has to be in the blood. A farmer has a way of standing on one leg and looking at a thing that isn't there. It sounds simple, but there is knack in it. The farmer is not surprised it is not there. He never expected it to be there. It is one of those things that ought to be, and is not. The farmer's life is full of such. Suffering reduced to a science is what the farmer stands for. All his life he is the good man struggling against adversity. Nothing his way comes right. This does not seem to be his planet. Providence means well, but she does not understand farming. She is doing her best, he supposes; that she is a born muddler is not her fault. If Providence could only step down for a month or two and take a few lessons in practical farming, things might be better; but this being out of the question there is nothing more to be said. From conversation with farmers one conjures up a picture of Providence as a well-intentioned amateur, put into a position for which she is utterly unsuited.

"Rain," says Providence, "they are wanting rain. What did I do with that rain?"

She finds the rain and starts it, and is pleased with herself until some Wandering Spirit pauses on his way and asks her sarcastically what she thinks she's doing.

"Raining," explains Providence. "They wanted rain—farmers, you know, that sort of people."

"They won't want anything for long," retorts the Spirit. "They'll be drowned in their beds before you've done with them."

"Don't say that!" says Providence.

"Well, have a look for yourself if you won't believe me," says the Spirit. "You've spoilt that harvest again, you've ruined all the fruit, and you are rotting even the turnips. Don't you ever learn by experience?"

"It is so difficult," says Providence, "to regulate these things just right."

"So it seems—for you," retorts the Spirit. "Anyhow, I should not rain any more, if I were you. If you must, at least give them time to build another ark." And the Wandering Spirit continues on his way.

"The place does look a bit wet, now I come to notice it," says Providence, peeping down over the edge of her star. "Better turn on the fine weather, I suppose."

She starts with she calls "set fair," and feeling now that she is something like a Providence, composes herself for a doze. She is startled out of her sleep by the return of the Wandering Spirit.

"Been down there again?" she asks him pleasantly.

"Just come back," explains the Wandering Spirit.

"Pretty spot, isn't it?" says Providence. "Things nice and dry down there now, aren't they?"

"You've hit it," he answers. "Dry is the word. The rivers are dried up, the wells are dried up, the cattle are dying, the grass is all withered. As for the harvest, there won't be any harvest for the next two years! Oh, yes, things are dry enough."

One imagines Providence bursting into tears. "But you suggested yourself a little fine weather."

"I know I did," answers the Spirit. "I didn't suggest a six months' drought with the thermometer at a hundred and twenty in the shade. Doesn't seem to me that you've got any sense at all."

"I do wish this job had been given to someone else," says Providence.

"Yes, and you are not the only one to wish it," retorts the Spirit unfeelingly.

"I do my best," urges Providence, wiping her eyes with her wings. "I am not fitted for it."

"A truer word you never uttered," retorts the Spirit.

"I try—nobody could try harder," wails Providence. "Everything I do seems to be wrong."

"What you want," says the Spirit, "is less enthusiasm and a little commonsense in place of it. You get excited, and then you lose your head. When you do send rain, ten to one you send it when it isn't wanted. You keep back your sunshine—just as a duffer at whist keeps back his trumps—until it is no good, and then you deal it out all at once."

"I'll try again," said Providence. "I'll try quite hard this time."

"You've been trying again," retorts the Spirit unsympathetically, "ever since I have known you. It is not that you do not try. It is that you have not got the hang of things. Why don't you get yourself an almanack?"

The Wandering Spirit takes his leave. Providence tells herself she really must get that almanack. She ties a knot in her handkerchief. It is not her fault: she was made like it. She forgets altogether for what reason she tied that knot. Thinks it was to remind her to send frosts in May, or Scotch mists in August. She is not sure which, so sends both. The farmer has ceased even to be angry with her—recognises that affliction and sorrow are good for his immortal soul, and pursues his way in calmness to the Bankruptcy Court.

Hubert St. Leonard, of Windrush Bottom Farm, I found to be a worried-looking gentleman. He taps his weather-glass, and hopes and fears, not knowing as yet that all things have been ordered for his ill. It will be years before his spirit is attuned to that attitude of tranquil despair essential to the farmer: one feels it. He is tall and thin, with a sensitive, mobile face, and a curious trick of taking his head every now and again between his hands, as if to be sure it is still there. When I met him he was on the point of starting for his round, so I walked with him. He told me that he had not always been a farmer. Till a few years ago he had been a stockbroker. But he had always hated his office; and having saved a little, had determined when he came to forty to enjoy the rare luxury of living his own life. I asked him if he found that farming paid. He said:

"As in everything else, it depends upon the price you put upon yourself. Now, as a casual observer, what wage per annum would you say I was worth?"

It was an awkward question.

"You are afraid that if you spoke candidly you would offend me," he suggested. "Very well. For the purpose of explaining my theory let us take, instead, your own case. I have read all your books, and I like them. Speaking as an admirer, I should estimate you at five hundred a year. You, perhaps, make two thousand, and consider yourself worth five."

The whimsical smile with which he accompanied the speech disarmed me.

"What we most of us do," he continued, "is to over-capitalise ourselves. John Smith, honestly worth a hundred a year, claims to be worth two. Result: difficulty of earning dividend, over-work, over-worry, constant fear of being wound up. Now, there is that about your work that suggests to me you would be happier earning five hundred a year than you ever will be earning two thousand. To pay your dividend—to earn your two thousand—you have to do work that brings you no pleasure in the doing. Content with five hundred, you could afford to do only that work that does give you pleasure. This is not a perfect world, we must remember. In the perfect world the thinker would be worth more than the mere jester. In the perfect world the farmer would be worth more than the stockbroker. In making the exchange I had to write myself down. I earn less money, but get more enjoyment out of life. I used to be able to afford champagne, but my liver was always wrong, and I dared not drink it. Now I cannot afford champagne, but I enjoy my beer. That is my theory, that we are all of us entitled to payment according to our market value, neither more nor less. You can take it all in cash. I used to. Or you can take less cash and more fun: that is what I am getting now."

"It is delightful," I said, "to meet with a philosopher. One hears about them, of course; but I had got it into my mind they were all dead."

"People laugh at philosophy," he said. "I never could understand why. It is the science of living a free, peaceful, happy existence. I would give half my remaining years to be a philosopher."

"I am not laughing at philosophy," I said. "I honestly thought you were a philosopher. I judged so from the way you talked."

"Talked!" he retorted. "Anybody can talk. As you have just said, I talk like a philosopher."

"But you not only talk," I insisted, "you behave like a philosopher. Sacrificing your income to the joy of living your own life! It is the act of a philosopher."

I wanted to keep him in good humour. I had three things to talk to him about: the cow, the donkey, and Dick.

"No, it wasn't," he answered. "A philosopher would have remained a stockbroker and been just as happy. Philosophy does not depend upon environment. You put the philosopher down anywhere. It is all the same to him, he takes his philosophy with him. You can suddenly tell him he is an emperor, or give him penal servitude for life. He goes on being a philosopher just as if nothing had happened. We have an old tom-cat. The children lead it an awful life. It does not seem to matter to the cat. They shut it up in the piano: their idea is that it will make a noise and frighten someone. It doesn't make a noise; it goes to sleep. When an hour later someone opens the piano, the poor thing is lying there stretched out upon the keyboard purring to itself. They dress it up in the baby's clothes and take it out in the perambulator: it lies there perfectly contented looking round at the scenery—takes in the fresh air. They haul it about by its tail. You would think, to watch it swinging gently to and fro head downwards, that it was grateful to them for giving it a new sensation. Apparently it looks on everything that comes its way as helpful experience. It lost a leg last winter in a trap: it goes about quite cheerfully on three. Seems to be rather pleased, if anything, at having lost the fourth—saves washing. Now, he is your true philosopher, that cat; never minds what happens to him, and is equally contented if it doesn't."

I found myself becoming fretful. I know a man with whom it is impossible to disagree. Men at the Club—new-comers—have been lured into taking bets that they could on any topic under the sun find themselves out of sympathy with him. They have denounced Mr. Lloyd George as a traitor to his country. This man has risen and shaken them by the hand, words being too weak to express his admiration of their outspoken fearlessness. You might have thought them Nihilists denouncing the Russian Government from the steps of the Kremlin at Moscow. They have, in the next breath, abused Mr. Balfour in terms transgressing the law of slander. He has almost fallen on their necks. It has transpired that the one dream of his life was to hear Mr. Balfour abused. I have talked to him myself for a quarter of an hour, and gathered that at heart he was a peace-at-any-price man, strongly in favour of Conscription, a vehement Republican, with a deep-rooted contempt for the working classes. It is not bad sport to collect half a dozen and talk round him. At such times he suggests the family dog that six people from different parts of the house are calling to at the same time. He wants to go to them all at once.

I felt I had got to understand this man, or he would worry me.

"We are going to be neighbours," I said, "and I am inclined to think I shall like you. That is, if I can get to know you. You commence by enthusing on philosophy: I hasten to agree with you. It is a noble science. When my youngest daughter has grown up, when the other one has learnt a little sense, when Dick is off my hands, and the British public has come to appreciate good literature, I am hoping to be a bit of a philosopher myself. But before I can explain to you my views you have already changed your own, and are likening the philosopher to an old tom-cat that seems to be weak in his head. Soberly now, what are you?"

"A fool," he answered promptly; "a most unfortunate fool. I have the mind of a philosopher coupled to an intensely irritable temperament. My philosophy teaches me to be ashamed of my irritability, and my irritability makes my philosophy appear to be arrant nonsense to myself. The philosopher in me tells me it does not matter when the twins fall down the wishing-well. It is not a deep well. It is not the first time they have fallen into it: it will not be the last. Such things pass: the philosopher only smiles. The man in me calls the philosopher a blithering idiot for saying it does not matter when it does matter. Men have to be called away from their work to haul them out. We all of us get wet. I get wet and excited, and that always starts my liver. The children's clothes are utterly spoilt. Confound them,"—the blood was mounting to his head—"they never care to go near the well except they are dressed in their best clothes. On other days they will stop indoors and read Foxe's 'Book of Martyrs.' There is something uncanny about twins. What is it? Why should twins be worse than other children? The ordinary child is not an angel, Heaven knows. Take these boots of mine. Look at them; I have had them for over two years. I tramp ten miles a day in them; they have been soaked through a hundred times. You buy a boy a pair of boots—"

"Why don't you cover over the well?" I suggested.

"There you are again," he replied. "The philosopher in me—the sensible man—says, 'What is the good of the well? It is nothing but mud and rubbish. Something is always falling into it—if it isn't the children it's the pigs. Why not do away with it?'"

"Seems to be sound advice," I commented.

"It is," he agreed. "No man alive has more sound commonsense than I have, if only I were capable of listening to myself. Do you know why I don't brick in that well? Because my wife told me I would have to. It was the first thing she said when she saw it. She says it again every time anything does fall into it. 'If only you would take my advice'—you know the sort of thing. Nobody irritates me more than the person who says, 'I told you so.' It's a picturesque old ruin: it used to be haunted. That's all been knocked on the head since we came. What self-respecting nymph can haunt a well into which children and pigs are for ever flopping?"

He laughed; but before I could join him he was angry again. "Why should I block up an historic well, that is an ornament to the garden, because a pack of fools can't keep a gate shut? As for the children, what they want is a thorough good whipping, and one of these days—"

A voice crying to us to stop interrupted him.

"Am on my round. Can't come," he shouted.

"But you must," explained the voice.

He turned so quickly that he almost knocked me over. "Bother and confound them all!" he said. "Why don't they keep to the time-table? There's no system in this place. That is what ruins farming—want of system."

He went on grumbling as he walked. I followed him. Halfway across the field we met the owner of the voice. She was a pleasant-looking lass, not exactly pretty—not the sort of girl one turns to look at in a crowd—yet, having seen her, it was agreeable to continue looking at her. St. Leonard introduced me to her as his eldest daughter, Janie, and explained to her that behind the study door, if only she would take the trouble to look, she would find a time-table—

"According to which," replied Miss Janie, with a smile, "you ought at the present moment to be in the rick-yard, which is just where I want you."

"What time is it?" he asked, feeling his waistcoat for a watch that appeared not to be there.

"Quarter to eleven," I told him.

He took his head between his hands. "Good God!" he cried, "you don't say that!"

The new binder, Miss Janie told us, had just arrived. She was anxious her father should see it was in working order before the men went back. "Otherwise," so she argued, "old Wilkins will persist it was all right when he delivered it, and we shall have no remedy."

We turned towards the house.

"Speaking of the practical," I said, "there were three things I came to talk to you about. First and foremost, that cow."

"Ah, yes, the cow," said St. Leonard. He turned to his daughter. "It was Maud, was it not?"

"No," she answered, "it was Susie."

"It is the one," I said, "that bellows most all night and three parts of the day. Your boy Hopkins thinks maybe she's fretting."

"Poor soul!" said St. Leonard. "We only took her calf away from her—when did we take her calf away from her?" he asked of Janie.

"On Thursday morning," returned Janie; "the day we sent her over."

"They feel it so at first," said St. Leonard sympathetically.

"It sounds a brutal sentiment," I said, "but I was wondering if by any chance you happened to have by you one that didn't feel it quite so much. I suppose among cows there is no class that corresponds to what we term our 'Smart Set'—cows that don't really care for their calves, that are glad to get away from them?"

Miss Janie smiled. When she smiled, you felt you would do much to see her smile again.

"But why not keep it up at your house, in the paddock," she suggested, "and have the milk brought down? There is an excellent cowshed, and it is only a mile away."

It struck me there was sense in this idea. I had not thought of that. I asked St. Leonard what I owed him for the cow. He asked Miss Janie, and she said sixteen pounds. I had been warned that in doing business with farmers it would be necessary always to bargain; but there was that about Miss Janie's tone telling me that when she said sixteen pounds she meant sixteen pounds. I began to see a brighter side to Hubert St. Leonard's career as a farmer.

"Very well," I said; "we will regard the cow as settled."

I made a note: "Cow, sixteen pounds. Have the cowshed got ready, and buy one of those big cans on wheels."

"You don't happen to want milk?" I put it to Miss Janie. "Susie seems to be good for about five gallons a day. I'm afraid if we drink it all ourselves we'll get too fat."

"At twopence halfpenny a quart, delivered at the house, as much as you like," replied Miss Janie.

I made a note of that also. "Happen to know a useful boy?" I asked Miss Janie.

"What about young Hopkins," suggested her father.

"The only male thing on this farm—with the exception of yourself, of course, father dear—that has got any sense," said Miss Janie. "He can't have Hopkins."

"The only fault I have to find with Hopkins," said St. Leonard, "is that he talks too much."

"Personally," I said, "I should prefer a country lad. I have come down here to be in the country. With Hopkins around, I don't somehow feel it is the country. I might imagine it a garden city: that is as near as Hopkins would allow me to get. I should like myself something more suggestive of rural simplicity."

"I think I know the sort of thing you mean," smiled Miss Janie. "Are you fairly good-tempered?"

"I can generally," I answered, "confine myself to sarcasm. It pleases me, and as far as I have been able to notice, does neither harm nor good to anyone else."

"I'll send you up a boy," promised Miss Janie.

I thanked her. "And now we come to the donkey."

"Nathaniel," explained Miss Janie, in answer to her father's look of enquiry. "We don't really want it."

"Janie," said Mr. St. Leonard in a tone of authority, "I insist upon being honest."

"I was going to be honest," retorted Miss Janie, offended.

"My daughter Veronica has given me to understand," I said, "that if I buy her this donkey it will be, for her, the commencement of a new and better life. I do not attach undue importance to the bargain, but one never knows. The influences that make for reformation in human character are subtle and unexpected. Anyhow, it doesn't seem right to throw a chance away. Added to which, it has occurred to me that a donkey might be useful in the garden."

"He has lived at my expense for upwards of two years," replied St. Leonard. "I cannot myself see any moral improvement he has brought into my family. What effect he may have upon your children, I cannot say. But when you talk about his being useful in a garden—"

"He draws a cart," interrupted Miss Janie.

"So long as someone walks beside him feeding him with carrots. We tried fixing the carrot on a pole six inches beyond his reach. That works all right in the picture: it starts this donkey kicking."

"You know yourself," he continued with growing indignation, "the very last time your mother took him out she used up all her carrots getting there, with the result that he and the cart had to be hauled home behind a trolley."

We had reached the yard. Nathaniel was standing with his head stretched out above the closed half of his stable door. I noticed points of resemblance between him and Veronica herself: there was about him a like suggestion of resignation, of suffering virtue misunderstood; his eye had the same wistful, yearning expression with which Veronica will stand before the window gazing out upon the purple sunset, while people are calling to her from distant parts of the house to come and put her things away. Miss Janie, bending over him, asked him to kiss her. He complied, but with a gentle, reproachful look that seemed to say, "Why call me back again to earth?"

It made me mad with him. I was wrong in thinking Miss Janie not a pretty girl. Hers is that type of beauty that escapes attention by its own perfection. It is the eccentric, the discordant, that arrests the roving eye. To harmony one has to attune oneself.

"I believe," said Miss Janie, as she drew away, wiping her cheek, "one could teach that donkey anything."

Apparently she regarded willingness to kiss her as indication of exceptional amiability.

"Except to work," commented her father. "I'll tell you what I'll do," he said. "If you take that donkey off my hands and promise not to send it back again, why, you can have it."

"For nothing?" demanded Janie woefully.

"For nothing," insisted her father. "And if I have any argument, I'll throw in the cart."

Miss Janie sighed and shrugged her shoulders. It was arranged that Hopkins should deliver Nathaniel into my keeping some time the next day. Hopkins, it appeared, was the only person on the farm who could make the donkey go.

"I don't know what it is," said St. Leonard, "but he has a way with him."

"And now," I said, "there remains but Dick."

"The lad I saw yesterday?" suggested St. Leonard. "Good-looking young fellow."

"He is a nice boy," I said. "I don't really think I know a nicer boy than Dick; and clever, when you come to understand him. There is only one fault I have to find with Dick: I don't seem able to get him to work."

Miss Janie was smiling. I asked her why.

"I was thinking," she answered, "how close the resemblance appears to be between him and Nathaniel."

It was true. I had not thought of it.

"The mistake," said St. Leonard, "is with ourselves. We assume every boy to have the soul of a professor, and every girl a genius for music. We pack off our sons to cram themselves with Greek and Latin, and put our daughters down to strum at the piano. Nine times out of ten it is sheer waste of time. They sent me to Cambridge, and said I was lazy. I was not lazy. I was not intended by nature for a Senior Wrangler. I did not see the good of being a Senior Wrangler. Who wants a world of Senior

Wranglers? Then why start every young man trying? I wanted to be a farmer. If intelligent lads were taught farming as a business, farming would pay. In the name of commonsense—"

"I am inclined to agree with you," I interrupted him. "I would rather see Dick a good farmer than a third-rate barrister, anyhow. He thinks he could take an interest in farming. There are ten weeks before he need go back to Cambridge, sufficient time for the experiment. Will you take him as a pupil?"

St. Leonard grasped his head between his hands and held it firmly. "If I consent," he said, "I must insist on being honest."

I saw the woefulness again in Janie's eyes.

"I think," I said, "it is my turn to be honest. I have got the donkey for nothing; I insist on paying for Dick. They are waiting for you in the rick-yard. I will settle the terms with Miss Janie."

He regarded us both suspiciously.

"I will promise to be honest," laughed Miss Janie.

"If it's more than I'm worth," he said, "I'll send him home again. My theory is—"

He stumbled over a pig which, according to the time-table, ought not to have been there. They went off hurriedly together, the pig leading, both screaming.

Miss Janie said she would show me the short cut across the fields; we could talk as we went. We walked in silence for awhile.

"You must not think," she said, "I like being the one to do all the haggling. I feel a little sore about it very often. But somebody, of course, must do it; and as for father, poor dear—"

I looked at her. Her's is the beauty to which a touch of sadness adds a charm.

"How old are you?" I asked her.

"Twenty," she answered, "next birthday."

"I judged you to be older," I said.

"Most people do," she answered.

"My daughter Robina," I said, "is just the same age—according to years; and Dick is twenty-one. I hope you will be friends with them. They have got sense, both of them. It comes out every now and again and surprises you. Veronica, I think, is nine. I am not sure how Veronica is going to turn out. Sometimes things happen that make us think she has a beautiful character, and then for quite long periods she seems to lose it altogether. The Little Mother—I don't know why we always call her Little Mother—will not join us till things are more ship-shape. She does not like to be thought an invalid, and if we have her about anywhere near work that has to be done, and are not always watching her, she gets at it and tires herself."

"I am glad we are going to be neighbours," said Miss Janie. "There are ten of us altogether. Father, I am sure, you will like; clever men always like father. Mother's day is Friday. As a rule it is the only day no one ever calls." She laughed. The cloud had vanished. "They come on other days and find us all in our old clothes. On Friday afternoon we sit in state and nobody comes near us, and we have to eat the cakes ourselves. It makes her so cross. You will try and remember Fridays, won't you?"

I made a note of it then and there.

"I am the eldest," she continued, "as I think father told you. Harry and Jack came next; but Jack is in Canada and Harry died, so there is somewhat of a gap between me and the rest. Bertie is twelve and Ted eleven; they are home just now for the holidays. Sally is eight, and then there come the twins. People don't half believe the tales that are told about twins, but I am sure there is no need to exaggerate. They are only six, but they have a sense of humour you would hardly credit. One is a boy, and the other a girl. They are always changing clothes, and we are never quite sure which is which. Wilfrid gets sent to bed because Winnie has not practised her scales, and Winnie is given syrup of squills because Wilfried has been eating green gooseberries. Last spring Winnie had the measles. When the doctor came on the fifth day he was as pleased as punch; he said it was the quickest cure he had ever known, and that really there was no reason why she might not get up. We had our suspicions, and they were right. Winnie was hiding in the cupboard, wrapped up in a blanket. They don't seem to mind what trouble they get into, provided it isn't their own. The only safe plan, unless you happen to catch them red-handed, is to divide the punishment between them, and leave them to settle accounts between themselves afterwards. Algy is four; till last year he was always called the baby. Now, of course, there is no excuse; but the name still clings to him in spite of his indignant protestations. Father called upstairs to him the other day: 'Baby, bring me down my gaiters.' He walked straight up to the cradle and woke up the baby. 'Get up,' I heard him say—I was just outside the door—'and take your father down his gaiters. Don't you hear him calling you?' He is a droll little fellow. Father took him to Oxford last Saturday. He is small for his age. The ticket-collector, quite contented, threw him a glance, and merely as a matter of form asked if he was under three. 'No,' he shouted before father could reply; 'I 'sists on being honest. I'se four.' It is father's pet phrase."

"What view do you take of the exchange," I asked her, "from stockbroking with its larger income to farming with its smaller?"

"Perhaps it was selfish," she answered, "but I am afraid I rather encouraged father. It seems to me mean, making your living out of work that does no good to anyone. I hate the bargaining, but the farming itself I love. Of course, it means having only one evening dress a year and making that myself. But even when I had a lot I always preferred wearing the one that I thought suited me the best. As for the children, they are as healthy as young savages, and everything they want to make them happy is just outside the door. The boys won't go to college; but seeing they will have to earn their own living, that, perhaps, is just as well. It is mother, poor dear, that worries so." She laughed again. "Her favourite walk is to the workhouse. She came back quite excited the other day because she had heard the Guardians intend to try the experiment of building separate houses for old married couples. She is convinced she and father are going to end their days there."

"You, as the business partner," I asked her, "are hopeful that the farm will pay?"

"Oh, yes," she answered, "it will pay all right—it does pay, for the matter of that. We live on it and live comfortably. But, of course, I can see mother's point of view, with seven young children to bring up. And it is not only that." She stopped herself abruptly. "Oh, well," she continued with a laugh, "you have got to know us. Father is trying. He loves experiments, and a woman hates experiments. Last year it was bare feet. I daresay it is healthier. But children who have been about in bare feet all the morning—well, it isn't pleasant when they sit down to lunch; I don't care what you say. You can't be always washing. He is so unpractical. He was quite angry with mother and myself because we wouldn't. And a man in bare feet looks so ridiculous. This summer it is short hair and no hats; and Sally had such pretty hair. Next year it will be sabots or turbans— something or other suggesting the idea that we've lately escaped from a fair. On Mondays and Thursdays we talk French. We have got a French nurse; and those are the only days in the week on which she doesn't understand a word that's said to her. We can none of us understand father, and that makes him furious. He won't say it in English; he makes a note of it, meaning to tell us on Tuesday or Friday, and then, of course, he forgets, and wonders why we haven't done it. He's the dearest fellow alive. When I think of him as a big boy, then he is charming, and if he really were only a big boy there are times when I would shake him and feel better for it."

She laughed again. I wanted her to go on talking, because her laugh was so delightful. But we had reached the road, and she said she must go back: there were so many things she had to do.

"We have not settled about Dick," I reminded her.

"Mother took rather a liking to him," she murmured.

"If Dick could make a living," I said, "by getting people to like him, I should not be so anxious about his future—lazy young devil!"

"He has promised to work hard if you let him take up farming," said Miss Janie.

"He has been talking to you?" I said.

She admitted it.

"He will begin well," I said. "I know him. In a month he will have tired of it, and be clamouring to do something else."

"I shall be very disappointed in him if he does," she said.

"I will tell him that," I said, "it may help. People don't like other people to be disappointed in them."

"I would rather you didn't," she said. "You could say that father will be disappointed in him. Father formed rather a good opinion of him, I know."

"I will tell him," I suggested, "that we shall all be disappointed in him."

She agreed to that, and we parted. I remembered, when she was gone, that after all we had not settled terms.

Dick overtook me a little way from home.

"I have settled your business," I told him.

"It's awfully good of you," said Dick.

"Mind," I continued, "it's on the understanding that you throw yourself into the thing and work hard. If you don't, I shall be disappointed in you, I tell you so frankly."

"That's all right, governor," he answered cheerfully. "Don't you worry."

"Mr. St. Leonard will also be disappointed in you, Dick," I informed him. "He has formed a very high opinion of you. Don't give him cause to change it."

"I'll get on all right with him," answered Dick. "Jolly old duffer, ain't he?"

"Miss Janie will also be disappointed in you," I added.

"Did she say that?" he asked.

"She mentioned it casually," I explained: "though now I come to think of it she asked me not to say so. What she wanted me to impress upon you was that her father would be disappointed in you."

Dick walked beside me in silence for awhile.

"Sorry I've been a worry to you, dad," he said at last

"Glad to hear you say so," I replied.

"I'm going to turn over a new leaf, dad," he said. "I'm going to work hard."

"About time," I said.

VI

We had cold bacon for lunch that day. There was not much of it. I took it to be the bacon we had not eaten for breakfast. But on a clean dish with parsley it looked rather neat. It did not suggest, however, a lunch for four people, two of whom had been out all the morning in the open air. There was some excuse for Dick.

"I never heard before," said Dick, "of cold fried bacon as a *hors d'œuvre*."

"It is not a *hors d'œuvre*," explained Robina. "It is all there is for lunch." She spoke in the quiet, passionless voice of one who has done with all human emotion. She added that she should not be requiring any herself, she having lunched already.

Veronica, conveying by her tone and bearing the impression of something midway between a perfect lady and a Christian martyr, observed that she also had lunched.

"Wish I had," growled Dick.

I gave him a warning kick. I could see he was on the way to getting himself into trouble. As I explained to him afterwards, a woman is most dangerous when at her meekest. A man, when he feels his temper rising, takes every opportunity of letting it escape. Trouble at such times he welcomes. A broken boot-lace, or a shirt without a button, is to him then as water in the desert. An only collar-stud that will disappear as if by magic from between his thumb and finger and vanish apparently into thin air is a piece of good fortune sent on these occasions only to those whom the gods love. By the time he has waddled on his hands and knees twice round the room, broken the boot-jack raking with it underneath the wardrobe, been bumped and slapped and kicked by every piece of furniture that the room contains, and ended up by stepping on that stud and treading it flat, he has not a bitter or an angry thought left in him. All that remains of him is sweet and peaceful. He fastens his collar with a safety-pin, humming an old song the while.

Failing the gifts of Providence, the children—if in health—can generally be depended upon to afford him an opening. Sooner or later one or another of them will do something that no child, when he was a boy, would have dared—or dreamed of daring—to even so much as think of doing. The child, conveying by expression that the world, it is glad to say, is slowly but steadily growing in sense, and pity it is that old-fashioned folks can't bustle up and keep abreast of it, points out that firstly it has not done this thing, that for various reasons—a few only of which need be dwelt upon—it is impossible it could have done this thing; that secondly it has been expressly requested to do this thing, that wishful always to give satisfaction, it has—at sacrifice of all its own ideas—gone out of its way to do this thing; that thirdly it can't help doing this thing, strive against fate as it will.

He says he does not want to hear what the child has got to say on the subject—nor on any other subject, neither then nor at any other time. He says there's going to be a new departure in this house, and that things all round are going to be very different. He suddenly remembers every rule and regulation he has made during the past ten years for the guidance of everybody, and that everybody, himself included, has forgotten. He tries to talk about them all at once, in haste lest he should forget them again. By the time he has succeeded in getting himself, if nobody else, to understand himself, the children are swarming round his knees extracting from him promises that in his sober moments he will be sorry that he made.

I knew a woman—a wise and good woman she was—who when she noticed that her husband's temper was causing him annoyance, took pains to help him to get rid of it. To relieve his sufferings I have known her search the house for a last month's morning paper and, ironing it smooth, lay it warm and neatly folded on his breakfast plate.

"One thing in this world to be thankful for, at all events, and that is that we don't live in Ditchley-in-the-Marsh," he would growl ten minutes later from the other side of it.

"Sounds a bit damp," the good woman would reply.

"Damp!" he would grunt, "who minds a bit of damp! Good for you. Makes us Englishmen what we are. Being murdered in one's bed about once a week is what I should object to."

"Do they do much of that sort of thing down there?" the good woman would enquire.

"Seems to be the chief industry of the place. Do you mean to say you don't remember that old maiden lady being murdered by her own gardener and buried in the fowl-run? You women! you take no interest in public affairs."

"I do remember something about it, now you mention it, dear," the good woman would confess. "Always seems such an innocent type of man, a gardener."

"Seems to be a special breed of them at Ditchley-in-the-Marsh," he answers. "Here again last Monday," he continues, reading with growing interest. "Almost the same case—even to the pruning knife. Yes, hanged if he doesn't!—buries her in the fowl-run. This is most extraordinary."

"It must be the imitative instinct asserting itself," suggests the good woman. "As you, dear, have so often pointed out, one crime makes another."

"I have always said so," he agrees; "it has always been a theory of mine."

He folds the paper over. "Dull dogs, these political chaps!" he says. "Here's the Duke of Devonshire, speaking last night at Hackney, begins by telling a funny story he says he has just heard about a parrot. Why, it's the same story somebody told a month ago; I remember reading it. Yes—upon my soul—word for word, I'd swear to it. Shows you the sort of men we're governed by."

"You can't expect everyone, dear, to possess your repertoire," the good woman remarks.

"Needn't say he's just heard it that afternoon, anyhow," responds the good man.

He turns to another column. "What the devil! Am I going off my head?" He pounces on the eldest boy. "When was the Oxford and Cambridge Boat-race?" he fiercely demands.

"The Oxford and Cambridge Boat-race!" repeats the astonished youth. "Why, it's over. You took us all to see it, last month. The Saturday before—"

The conversation for the next ten minutes he conducts himself, unaided. At the end he is tired, maybe a trifle hoarse. But all his bad temper is gone. His sorrow is there was not sufficient of it. He could have done with more.

Woman knows nothing of simple mechanics. A woman thinks you can get rid of steam by boxing it up and sitting on the safety-valve.

"Feeling as I do this morning, that I'd like to wring everybody's neck for them," the average woman argues to herself; "my proper course—I see it clearly—is to creep about the house, asking of everyone that has the time to spare to trample on me."

She coaxes you to tell her of her faults. When you have finished she asks for more—reminds you of one or two you had missed out. She wonders why it is that she is always wrong. There must be a reason for it; if only she could discover it. She wonders how it is that people can put up with her—thinks it so good of them.

At last, of course, the explosion happens. The awkward thing is that neither she herself nor anyone else knows when it is coming. A husband cornered me one evening in the club. It evidently did him good to talk. He told me that, finding his wife that morning in one of her rare listening moods, he had seized the opportunity to mention one or two matters in connection with the house he would like to have altered; that was, if she had no objection. She had—quite pleasantly—reminded him the house was his, that he was master there. She added that any wish of his of course was law to her.

He was a young and inexperienced husband; it seemed to him a hopeful opening. He spoke of quite a lot of things—things about which he felt that he was right and she was wrong. She went and fetched a quire of paper, and borrowed his pencil and wrote them down.

Later on, going through his letters in the study, he found an unexpected cheque; and ran upstairs and asked her if she would not like to come out with him and get herself a new hat.

"I could have understood it," he moaned, "if she had dropped on me while I was—well, I suppose, you might say lecturing her. She had listened to it like a lamb—hadn't opened her mouth except to say 'yes, dear,' or 'no, dear.' Then, when I only asked her if she'd like a new hat, she goes suddenly raving mad. I never saw a woman go so mad."

I doubt if there be anything in nature quite as unexpected as a woman's temper, unless it be tumbling into a hole. I told all this to Dick. I have told it him before. One of these days he will know it.

"You are right to be angry with me," Robina replied meekly; "there is no excuse for me. The whole thing is the result of my own folly."

Her pathetic humility should have appealed to him. He can be sympathetic, when he isn't hungry. Just then he happened to be hungry.

"I left you making a pie," he said. "It looked to me a fair-sized pie. There was a duck on the table, with a cauliflower and potatoes; Veronica was up to her elbows in peas. It made me hungry merely passing through the kitchen. I wouldn't have anything to eat in the town for fear of spoiling my appetite. Where is it all? You don't mean to say that you and Veronica have eaten the whole blessed lot!"

There is one thing—she admits it herself—that exhausts Veronica's patience: it is unjust suspicion.

"Do I look as if I'd eaten anything for hours and hours?" Veronica demanded. "You can feel my waistband if you don't believe me."

"You said just now you had had your lunch," Dick argued.

"I know I did," Veronica admitted. "One minute you are told that it is wicked to tell lies; the next—"

"Veronica!" Robina interrupted threateningly.

"It's easy for you," retorted Veronica. "You are not a growing child. You don't feel it."

"The least you can do," said Robina, "is to keep silence."

"What's the good," said Veronica—not without reason. "You'll tell them when I've gone to bed, and can't put in a word for myself. Everything is always my fault. I wish sometimes that I was dead."

"That I were dead," I corrected her. "The verb 'to wish,' implying uncertainty, should always be followed by the conditional mood."

"You ought," said Robina, "to be thankful to Providence that you're not dead."

"People are sorry when you're dead," said Veronica.

"I suppose there's some bread-and-cheese in the house," suggested Dick.

"The baker, for some reason or another, has not called this morning," Robina answered sweetly. "Neither unfortunately has the grocer. Everything there is to eat in the house you see upon the table."

"Accidents will happen," I said. "The philosopher—as our friend St. Leonard would tell us—only smiles."

"I could smile," said Dick, "if it were his lunch."

"Cultivate," I said, "a sense of humour. From a humorous point of view this lunch is rather good."

"Did you have anything to eat at the St. Leonards'?" he asked.

"Just a glass or so of beer and a sandwich or two," I admitted. "They brought it out to us while we were talking in the yard. To tell the truth, I was feeling rather peckish."

Dick made no answer, but continued to chew bacon-rind. Nothing I could say seemed to cheer him. I thought I would try religion.

"A dinner of herbs—the sentiment applies equally to lunch—and contentment therewith is better," I said, "than a stalled ox."

"Don't talk about oxen," he interrupted fretfully. "I feel I could just eat one—a plump one."

There is a man I know. I confess he irritates me. His argument is that you should always rise from a meal feeling hungry. As I once explained to him, you cannot rise from a meal feeling hungry without sitting down to a meal feeling hungry; which means, of course, that you are always hungry. He agreed with me. He said that was the idea—always ready.

"Most people," he said, "rise from a meal feeling no more interest in their food. That was a mental attitude injurious to digestion. Keep it always interested; that was the proper way to treat it."

"By 'it' you mean. . . ?" I said.

"Of course," he answered; "I'm talking about it."

"Now I myself," he explained—"I rise from breakfast feeling eager for my lunch. I get up from my lunch looking forward to my dinner. I go to bed just ready for my breakfast."

Cheerful expectancy, he said, was a wonderful aid to digestion. "I call myself," he said, "a cheerful feeder."

"You don't seem to me," I said, "to be anything else. You talk like a tadpole. Haven't you any other interest in life? What about home, and patriotism, and Shakespeare—all those sort of things? Why not give it a square meal, and silence it for an hour or two; leave yourself free to think of something else."

"How can you think of anything," he argued, "when your stomach's out of order?"

"How can you think of anything," I argued, "when it takes you all your time to keep it in order? You are not a man; you are a nurse to your own stomach." We were growing excited, both of us, forgetting our natural refinement. "You don't get even your one afternoon a week. You are healthy enough, I admit it. So are the convicts at Portland. They never suffer from indigestion. I knew a doctor once who prescribed for a patient two years' penal servitude as the only thing likely to do him permanent good. Your stomach won't let you smoke. It won't let you drink—not when you are thirsty. It allows you a glass of Apenta water at times when you don't want it, assuming there could ever be a time when you did want it. You are deprived of your natural victuals, and made to live upon prepared food, as though you were some sort of a prize chicken. You are sent to bed at eleven, and dressed in hygienic clothing that makes no pretence to fit you. Talk of being hen-pecked! Why, the mildest husband living would run away or drown himself, rather than remain tied for the rest of his existence to your stomach."

"It is easy to sneer," he said.

"I am not sneering," I said; "I am sympathising with you."

He said he did not want any sympathy. He said if only I would give up over-eating and drinking myself, it would surprise me how bright and intelligent I should become.

I thought this man might be of use to us on the present occasion. Accordingly I spoke of him and of his theory. Dick seemed impressed.

"Nice sort of man?" he asked.

"An earnest man," I replied. "He practises what he preaches, and whether because, or in spite of it, the fact remains that a chirpier soul I am sure does not exist."

"Married?" demanded Dick.

"A single man," I answered. "In all things an idealist. He has told me he will never marry until he can find his ideal woman."

"What about Robina here!" suggested Dick. "Seem to have been made for one another."

Robina smiled. It was a wan, pathetic smile.

"Even he," thought Robina, "would want his beans cooked to time, and to feel that a reasonable supply of nuts was always in the house. We incompetent women never ought to marry."

We had finished the bacon. Dick said he would take a stroll into the town. Robina suggested he might take Veronica with him, that perhaps a bun and a glass of milk would do the child no harm.

Veronica for a wonder seemed to know where all her things were. Before Dick had filled his pipe she was ready dressed and waiting for him. Robina said she would give them a list of things they might bring back with them. She also asked Dick to get together a plumber, a carpenter, a bricklayer, a glazier, and a civil engineer, and to see to it that they started off at once. She thought that among them they might be able to do all that was temporarily necessary, but the great thing was that the work should be commenced without delay.

"Why, what on earth's the matter, old girl?" asked Dick. "Have you had an accident?"

Then it was that Robina exploded. I had been wondering when it would happen. To Dick's astonishment it happened then.

Yes, she answered, there had been an accident. Did he suppose that seven scrimpy scraps of bacon was her notion of a lunch between four hungry persons? Did he, judging from himself, imagine that our family yielded only lunatics? Was it kind—was it courteous to his parents, to the mother he pretended to love, to the father whose grey hairs he was by his general behaviour bringing down in sorrow to the grave—to assume without further enquiry that their eldest daughter was an imbecile? (My hair, by-the-bye, is not grey. There may be a suggestion of greyness here and there, the natural result of deep thinking. To describe it in the lump as grey is to show lack of observation. And at forty-eight—or a trifle over—one is not going down into the grave, not straight down. Robina when excited uses exaggerated language. I did not, however, interrupt her; she meant well. Added to which, interrupting Robina, when—to use her own expression—she is tired of being a worm, is like trying to stop a cyclone with an umbrella.) Had his attention been less concentrated on the guzzling of cold bacon (he had only had four mouthfuls, poor fellow)—had he noticed the sweet patient child starving before his very eyes (this referred to Veronica)—his poor elder sister, worn out with work and worry, pining for nourishment herself, it might have occurred to even his intelligence that there had been an accident. The selfishness, the egotism of men it was that staggered, overwhelmed Robina, when she came to think of it.

Robina paused. Not for want of material, I judged, so much as want of breath. Veronica performed a useful service by seizing the moment to express a hope that it was not early-closing day. Robina felt a conviction that it was: it would be just like Dick to stand there dawdling in a corner till it was too late to do anything.

"I have been trying to get out of this corner for the last five minutes," explained Dick, with that angelic smile of his that I confess is irritating. "If you have done talking, and will give me an opening, I will go."

Robina told him that she had done talking. She gave him her reasons for having done talking. If talking to him would be of any use she would often have felt it her duty to talk to him, not only with regard to his stupidity and selfishness and general aggravatingness, but with reference to his character as a whole. Her excuse for not talking to him was the crushing conviction of the hopelessness of ever effecting any improvement in him. Were it otherwise—

"Seriously speaking," said Dick, now escaped from his corner, "something, I take it, has gone wrong with the stove, and you want a sort of general smith."

He opened the kitchen door and looked in.

"Great Scott!" he said. "What was it—an earthquake?"

I looked in over his shoulder.

"But it could not have been an earthquake," I said. "We should have felt it."

"It is not an earthquake," explained Robina. "It is your youngest daughter's notion of making herself useful."

Robina spoke severely. I felt for the moment as if I had done it all myself. I had an uncle who used to talk like that. "Your aunt," he would say, regarding me with a reproachful eye, "your aunt can be, when she likes, the most trying woman to live with I have ever known." It would depress me for days. I would wonder whether I ought to speak to her about it, or whether I should be doing only harm.

"But how did she do it?" I demanded. "It is impossible that a mere child—where is the child?"

The parlour contained but Robina. I hurried to the door; Dick was already half across the field. Veronica I could not see.

"We are making haste," Dick shouted back, "in case it is early-closing day."

"I want Veronica!" I shouted.

"What?" shouted Dick.

"Veronica!" I shouted with my hands to my mouth.

"Yes!" shouted Dick. "She's on ahead."

It was useless screaming any more. He was now climbing the stile.

"They always take each other's part, those two," sighed Robina.

"Yes, and you are just as bad," I told her; "if he doesn't, you do. And then if it's you they take your part. And you take his part. And he takes both your parts. And between you all I am just getting tired of bringing any of you up." (Which is the truth.) "How did this thing happen?"

"I had got everything finished," answered Robina. "The duck was in the oven with the pie; the peas and potatoes were boiling nicely. I was feeling hot, and I thought I could trust Veronica to watch the things for awhile. She promised not to play King Alfred."

"What's that?" I asked.

"You know," said Robina—"King Alfred and the cakes. I left her one afternoon last year when we were on the houseboat to watch some buns. When I came back she was sitting in front of the fire, wrapped up in the table-cloth, with Dick's banjo on her knees and a cardboard crown upon her head. The buns were all burnt to a cinder. As I told her, if I had known what she wanted to be up to I could have given her some extra bits of dough to make believe with. But oh, no! if you please, that would not have suited her at all. It was their being real buns, and my being real mad, that was the best part of the game. She is an uncanny child."

"What was the game this time?" I asked.

"I don't think it was intended for a game—not at first," answered Robina. "I went into the wood to pick some flowers for the table. I was on my way back, still at some distance from the house, when I heard quite a loud report. I took it for a gun, and wondered what anyone would be shooting in July. It must be rabbits, I thought. Rabbits never seem to have any time at all to themselves, poor things. And in consequence I did not hurry myself. It must have been about twenty minutes later when I came in sight of the house. Veronica was in the garden deep in confabulation with an awful-looking boy, dressed in nothing but rags. His face and hands were almost black. You never saw such an object. They both seemed very excited. Veronica came to meet me; and with a face as serious as mine is now, stood there and told me the most barefaced pack of lies you ever heard. She said that a few minutes after I had gone, robbers had come out of the wood—she talked about them as though there had been hundreds—and had with the most awful threats demanded to be admitted into the house. Why they had not lifted the latch and walked in, she did not explain. It appeared this cottage was their secret rendezvous, where all their treasure lies hidden. Veronica would not let them in, but shouted for help: and immediately this awful-looking boy, to whom she introduced me as 'Sir Robert' something or another, had appeared upon the scene; and then there had followed—well, I have not the patience to tell you the whole of the rigmarole they had concocted. The upshot of it was that the robbers, defeated in their attempt to get into the house, had fired a secret mine, which had exploded in the kitchen. If I did not believe them I could go into the kitchen and see for myself. Say what I would, that is the story they both stuck to. It was not till I had talked to Veronica for a quarter of an hour, and had told her that you would most certainly communicate with the police, and that she would have to convince a judge and jury of the truth of her story, that I got any sense at all out of her."

"What was the sense you did get out of her?" I asked.

"Well, I am not sure even now that it is the truth," said Robina—"the child does not seem to possess a proper conscience. What she will grow up like, if something does not happen to change her, it is awful to think."

"I don't want to appear a hustler," I said, "and maybe I am mistaken in the actual time, but it feels to me like hours since I asked you how the catastrophe really occurred."

"I am telling you," explained Robina, hurt. "She was in the kitchen yesterday when I mentioned to Harry's mother, who had looked in to help me wash up, that the kitchen chimney smoked: and then she said—"

"Who said?" I asked.

"Why, she did," answered Robina, "Harry's mother. She said that very often a pennyworth of gunpowder—"

"Now at last we have begun," I said. "From this point I may be able to help you, and we will get on. At the word 'gunpowder' Veronica pricked up her ears. The thing by its very nature would appeal to Veronica's sympathies. She went to bed dreaming of gunpowder. Left in solitude before the kitchen fire, other maidens might have seen pictured in the glowing coals, princes, carriages, and balls. Veronica saw visions of gunpowder. Who knows?—perhaps even she one day will have gunpowder of her own! She looks up from her reverie: a fairy godmamma in the disguise of a small boy—it was a small boy, was it not?"

"Rather a nice little boy, he gave me the idea of having been, originally," answered Robina; "the child, I should say, of well-to-do parents. He was dressed in a little Lord Fauntleroy suit—or rather, he had been."

"Did Veronica know how he was—anything about him?" I asked.

"Nothing that I could get out of her," replied Robina; "you know her way—how she chums on with anybody and everybody. As I told her, if she had been attending to her duties instead of staring out of the window, she would not have seen him. He happened to be crossing the field just at the time."

"A boy born to ill-luck, evidently," I observed. "To Veronica of course he seemed like the answer to a prayer. A boy would surely know where gunpowder could be culled."

"They must have got a pound of it from somewhere," said Robina, "judging from the result."

"Any notion where they got it from?" I asked.

"No," explained Robina. "All Veronica can say is that he told her he knew where he could get some, and was gone about ten minutes. Of course they must have stolen it—even that did not seem to trouble her."

"It came to her as a gift from the gods, Robina," I explained. "I remember how I myself used to feel about these things, at ten. To have enquired further would have seemed to her impious. How was it they were not both killed?"

"Providence," was Robina's suggestion: it seemed to be the only one possible. "They lifted off one of the saucepans and just dropped the thing in—fortunately wrapped up in a brown paper parcel, which gave them both time to get out of the house. At least Veronica got clear off. For a change it was not she who fell over the mat, it was the boy."

I looked again into the kitchen; then I returned and put my hands on Robina's shoulders. "It is a most amusing incident—as it has turned out," I said.

"It might have turned out rather seriously," thought Robina.

"It might," I agreed: "she might be lying upstairs."

"She is a wicked, heartless child," said Robina; "she ought to be punished."

I lent Robina my handkerchief; she never has one of her own.

"She is going to be punished," I said; "I will think of something."

"And so ought I," said Robina; "it was my fault, leaving her, knowing what she's like. I might have murdered her. She doesn't care. She's stuffing herself with cakes at this very moment."

"They will probably give her indigestion," I said. "I hope they do."

"Why didn't you have better children?" sobbed Robina; "we are none of us any good to you."

"You are not the children I wanted, I confess," I answered.

"That's a nice kind thing to say!" retorted Robina indignantly.

"I wanted such charming children," I explained—"my idea of charming children: the children I had imagined for myself. Even as babies you disappointed me."

Robina looked astonished.

"You, Robina, were the most disappointing," I complained. "Dick was a boy. One does not calculate upon boy angels; and by the time Veronica arrived I had got more used to things. But I was so excited when you came. The Little Mother and I would steal at night into the nursery. 'Isn't it wonderful,' the Little Mother would whisper, 'to think it all lies hidden there: the little tiresome child, the sweetheart they will one day take away from us, the wife, the mother?' 'I am glad it is a girl,' I would whisper; 'I shall be able to watch her grow into womanhood. Most of the girls one comes across in books strike one as not perhaps quite true to life. It will give me such an advantage having a girl of my own. I shall keep a note-book, with a lock and key, devoted to her.'"

"Did you?" asked Robina.

"I put it away," I answered; "there were but a few pages written on. It came to me quite early in your life that you were not going to be the model heroine. I was looking for the picture baby, the clean, thoughtful baby, with its magical, mystical smile. I wrote poetry about you, Robina, but you would slobber and howl. Your little nose was always having to be wiped, and somehow the poetry did not seem to fit you. You were at your best when you were asleep, but you would not even sleep when it was expected of you. I think, Robina, that the fellows who draw the pictures for the comic journals of the man in his night-shirt with the squalling baby in his arms must all be single men. The married man sees only sadness in the design. It is not the mere discomfort. If the little creature were ill or in pain we should not think of that. It is the reflection that we, who meant so well, have brought into the world just an ordinary fretful human creature with a nasty temper of its own: that is the tragedy, Robina. And then you grew into a little girl. I wanted the soulful little girl with the fathomless eyes, who would steal to me at twilight and question me concerning life's conundrums.

"But I used to ask you questions," grumbled Robina, "and you would tell me not to be silly."

"Don't you understand, Robina?" I answered. "I am not blaming you, I am blaming myself. We are like children who plant seeds in a garden, and then are angry with the flowers because they are not what we expected. You were a dear little girl; I see that now, looking back. But not the little girl I had in my mind. So I missed you, thinking of the little girl you were not. We do that all our lives, Robina. We are always looking for the flowers that do not grow, passing by, trampling underfoot, the blossoms round about us. It was the same with Dick. I wanted a naughty boy. Well, Dick was naughty, no one can say that he was not. But it was not my naughtiness. I was prepared for his robbing orchards. I rather hoped he would rob orchards. All the high-spirited boys in books rob orchards, and become great men. But there were not any orchards handy. We happened to be living in Chelsea at the time he ought to have been robbing orchards: that, of course, was my fault. I did not think of that. He stole a bicycle that a lady had left outside the tea-room in Battersea Park, he and another boy, the son of a common barber, who shaved people for three-halfpence. I am a Republican in theory, but it grieved me that a son of mine could be drawn to such companionship. They contrived to keep it for a week—till the police found it one night, artfully hidden behind bushes. Logically, I do not see why stealing apples should be noble and stealing bicycles should be mean, but it struck me that way at the time. It was not the particular steal I had been hoping for.

"I wanted him wild; the hero of the book was ever in his college days a wild young man. Well, he was wild. It cost me three hundred pounds to keep that breach of promise case out of Court; I had never imagined a breach of promise case. Then he got drunk, and bonneted a bishop in mistake for a 'bull-dog.' I didn't mind the bishop. That by itself would have been wholesome fun. But to think that a son of mine should have been drunk!"

"He has never been drunk since," pleaded Robina. "He had only three glasses of champagne and a liqueur: it was the liqueur—he was not used to it. He got into the wrong set. You cannot in college belong to the wild set without getting drunk occasionally."

"Perhaps not," I admitted. "In the book the wild young man drinks without ever getting drunk. Maybe there is a difference between life and the book. In the book you enjoy your fun, but contrive somehow to escape the licking: in life the licking is the only thing sure. It was the wild young man of fiction I was looking for, who, a fortnight before the exam., ties a wet towel round his head, drinks strong tea, and passes easily with honours. He tried the wet towel, he tells me. It never would keep in its place. Added to which it gave him neuralgia; while the strong tea gave him indigestion. I used to picture myself the proud, indulgent father lecturing him for his wildness—turning away at some point in the middle of my tirade to hide a smile. There was never any smile to hide. I feel that he has behaved disgracefully, wasting his time and my money."

"He is going to turn over a new leaf," said Robina: "I am sure he will make an excellent farmer."

"I did not want a farmer," I explained; "I wanted a Prime Minister. Children, Robina, are very disappointing. Veronica is all wrong. I like a mischievous child. I like reading stories of mischievous children: they amuse me. But not the child who puts a pound of gunpowder into a red-hot fire, and escapes with her life by a miracle."

"And yet, I daresay," suggested Robina, "that if one put it into a book—I mean that if you put it into a book, it would read amusingly."

"Likely enough," I agreed. "Other people's troubles can always be amusing. As it is, I shall be in a state of anxiety for the next six months, wondering, every moment that she is out of my sight, what new devilment she is up to. The Little Mother will be worried out of her life, unless we can keep it from her."

"Children will be children," murmured Robina, meaning to be comforting.

"That is what I am complaining of, Robina. We are always hoping that ours won't be. She is full of faults, Veronica, and they are not always nice faults. She is lazy—lazy is not the word for it."

"She is lazy," Robina was compelled to admit.

"There are other faults she might have had and welcome," I pointed out; "faults I could have taken an interest in and liked her all the better for. You children are so obstinate. You will choose your own faults. Veronica is not truthful always. I wanted a family of little George Washingtons, who could not tell a lie. Veronica can. To get herself out of trouble—and provided there is any hope of anybody believing her—she does."

"We all of us used to when we were young," Robina maintained; "Dick used to, I used to. It is a common fault with children."

"I know it is," I answered. "I did not want a child with common faults. I wanted something all my own. I wanted you, Robina, to be my ideal daughter. I had a girl in my mind that I am sure would have been charming. You are not a bit like her. I don't say she was perfect, she had her failings, but they were such delightful failings—much better than yours, Robina. She had a temper—a woman without a temper is insipid; but it was that kind of temper that made you love her all the more. Yours doesn't, Robina. I wish you had not been in such a hurry, and had left me to arrange your temper for you. We should all of us have preferred mine. It had all the attractions of temper without the drawbacks of the ordinary temper."

"Couldn't use it up, I suppose, for yourself, Pa?" suggested Robina.

"It was a lady's temper," I explained. "Besides," as I asked her, "what is wrong with the one I have?"

"Nothing," answered Robina. Yet her tone conveyed doubt. "It seems to me sometimes that an older temper would suit you better, that was all."

"You have hinted as much before, Robina," I remarked, "not only with reference to my temper, but with reference to things generally. One would think that you were dissatisfied with me because I am too young."

"Not in years perhaps," replied Robina, "but—well, you know what I mean. One wants one's father to be always great and dignified."

"We cannot change our ego," I explained to her. "Some daughters would appreciate a father youthful enough in temperament to sympathise with and to indulge them. The solemn old fogey you have in your mind would have brought you up very differently. Let me tell you that, my girl. You would not have liked him, if you had had him."

"Perhaps not," Robina agreed. "You are awfully good in some ways."

"What we have got to do in this world, Robina," I said, "is to take people as they are, and make the best of them. We cannot expect everybody to be just as we would have them, and maybe we should not like them any better if they were. Don't bother yourself about how much nicer they might be; think how nice they are."

Robina said she would try. I have hopes of making Robina a sensible woman.

VII

Dick and Veronica returned laden with parcels. They explained that "Daddy Slee," as it appeared he was generally called, a local builder of renown, was following in his pony-cart, and was kindly bringing the bulkier things with him.

"I tried to hustle him," said Dick, "but coming up after he had washed himself and had his tea seemed to be his idea of hustling. He has got the reputation of being an honest old Johnny, slow but sure; the others, they tell me, are slower. I thought you might care, later on, to talk to him about the house."

Veronica took off her things and put them away, each one in its proper place. She said, if no one wanted her, she would read a chapter of "The Vicar of Wakefield," and retired upstairs. Robina and I had an egg with our tea; Mr. Slee arrived as we had finished, and I took him straight into the kitchen. He was a large man, with a dreamy expression and a habit of sighing. He sighed when he saw our kitchen.

"There's four days' work for three men here," he said, "and you'll want a new stove. Lord! what trouble children can be!"

Robina agreed with him.

"Meanwhile," she demanded, "how am I to cook?"

"Myself, missie," sighed Mr. Slee, "I don't see how you are going to cook."

"We'll all have to tramp home again," thought Dick.

"And tell Little Mother the reason, and frighten her out of her life!" retorted Robina indignantly.

Robina had other ideas. Mr. Slee departed, promising that work should be commenced at seven o'clock on Monday morning. Robina, the door closed, began to talk.

"Let Pa have a sandwich," said Robina, "and catch the six-fifteen."

"We might all have a sandwich," suggested Dick; "I could do with one myself."

"Pa can explain," said Robina, "that he has been called back to town on business. That will account for everything, and Little Mother will not be alarmed."

"She won't believe that business has brought him back at nine o'clock on a Saturday night," argued Dick; "you think that Little Mother hasn't any sense. She'll see there's something up, and ask a hundred questions. You know what she is."

JEROME K. JEROME

"Pa," said Robina, "will have time while in the train to think out something plausible; that's where Pa is clever. With Pa off my hands I sha'n't mind. We three can live on cold ham and things like that. By Thursday we will be all right, and then he can come down again."

I pointed out to Robina, kindly but firmly, the utter absurdity of her idea. How could I leave them, three helpless children, with no one to look after them? What would the Little Mother say? What might not Veronica be up to in my absence? There were other things to be considered. The donkey might arrive at any moment—no responsible person there to receive him—to see to it that his simple wants would be provided for. I should have to interview Mr. St. Leonard again to fix up final details as regarded Dick. Who was going to look after the cow, about to be separated from us? Young Bute would be down again with plans. Who was going to take him over the house, explain things to him intelligibly? The new boy might turn up—this simple son of the soil Miss Janie had promised to dig out and send along. He would talk Berkshire. Who would there be to understand him— to reply to him in dialect? What was the use of her being impetuous and talking nonsense?

She went on cutting sandwiches. She said they were not helpless children. She said if she and Dick at forty-two hadn't grit enough to run a six-roomed cottage it was time they learned.

"Who's forty-two?" I demanded.

"We are," explained Robina, "Dick and I—between us. We shall be forty-two next birthday. Nearly your own age."

"Veronica," she continued, "for the next few days won't be a child at all. She knows nothing of the happy medium. She is either herself or she goes to the opposite extreme, and tries to be an angel. Till about the end of the week it will be like living with a vision. As for the donkey, we'll try and make him feel as much at home as if you were here."

"I don't mean to be rude, Pa," Robina explained, "but from the way you put it you evidently regard yourself as the only one among us capable of interesting him. I take it he won't mind for a night or two sharing the shed with the cow. If he looks shocked at the suggestion, Dick can knock up a partition. I'd rather for the present, till you come down again, the cow stopped where she was. She helps to wake me in the morning. You may reckon you have settled everything as far as Dick is concerned. If you talk to St. Leonard again for an hour it will be about the future of the Yellow Races or the possibility of life in Jupiter. If you mention terms he will be insulted, and if he won't let you then you will be insulted, and the whole thing will be off. Let me talk to Janie. We've both of us got sense. As for Mr. Bute, I know all your ideas about the house, and I sha'n't listen to any of his silly arguments. What that young man wants is someone to tell him what he's got to do, and then let there be an end of it. And the sooner that handy boy turns up the better. I don't mind what he talks. All I want him to do is to clean knives and fetch water and chop wood. At the worst I'll get that home to him by pantomime. For conversation he can wait till you come down."

That is the gist of what she said. It didn't run exactly as I have put it down. There were points at which I interrupted, but Robina never listens; she just talks on, and at the end she assumes that, as a matter of course, you have come round to her point of view, and persuading her that you haven't means beginning the whole thing over again.

She said I hadn't time to talk, and that she would write and tell me everything. Dick also said he would write and tell me everything; and that if I felt moved to send them down a hamper—the sort of thing that, left to themselves, Fortnum & Mason would put together for a good-class picnic, say, for six persons—I might rely upon it that nothing would be wasted.

Veronica, by my desire, walked with me to the end of the lane. I talked to her very seriously. Her difficulty was that she had not been blown up. Had she been blown up, then she would have known herself she had done wrong. In the book it is the disobedient child that is tossed by the bull. The child that has been sent with the little basket to visit the sick aunt may be right in the bull's way. That is a bit of bad luck for the bull. The poor bull is compelled to waste valuable time working round carefully, so as not to upset the basket. If the wicked child had sense (which in the book does not happen), it would, while the bull was dodging to get past the good child, seize the opportunity to move itself quickly. The wicked child never looks round, but pegs along steadily; and when the bull arrives it is sure to be in the most convenient position for receiving moral lessons. The good child, whatever its weight, crosses the ice in safety. The bad child may turn the scale at two stone lighter; the ice will have none of him. "Don't you talk to me about relative pressure to the square inch," says the indignant ice. "You were unkind to your little baby brother the week before last: in you go." Veronica's argument, temperately and courteously expressed, I admit, came practically to this:

"I may have acted without sufficient knowledge to guide me. My education has not, perhaps, on the whole, been ordered wisely. Subjects that I feel will never be of the slightest interest or consequence to me have been insisted upon with almost tiresome reiteration. Matters that should be useful and helpful to me—gunpowder, to take but one example—I have been left in ignorance concerning. About all that I say nothing; people have done their best according to their lights, no doubt. When, however, we come to purity of motives, singleness of intention, then, I maintain, I am above reproach. The proof of this is that Providence has bestowed upon me the seal of its approval: I was not blown up. Had my conduct been open to censure—as in certain quarters has been suggested—should I be walking besides you now, undamaged—not a hair turned, as the saying is? No. Discriminating Fate—that is, if any reliance at all is to be placed on literature for the young—would have made it her business that at least I was included in the *débris*. Instead, what do we notice!—a shattered chimney, a ruined stove, broken windows, a wreckage of household utensils; I, alone of all things, miraculously preserved. I do not wish to press the point offensively, but really it would almost seem that it must be you three—you, my dear parent, upon whom will fall the bill for repairs; Dick, apt to attach too much importance, maybe, to his victuals, and who for the next few days will be compelled to exist chiefly upon tinned goods; Robina, by nature of a worrying disposition, certain till things get straight again to be next door to off her head—who must, by reason of conduct into which I do not enquire, have merited chastisement at the hands of Providence. The moral lesson would certainly appear to be between you three. I—it grows clear to me—have been throughout but the innocent instrument."

Admit the premise that to be virtuous is to escape whipping, the argument is logical. I felt that left uncombated it might lead us into yet further trouble.

"Veronica," I said, "the time has come to reveal to you a secret: literature is not always a safe guide to life."

"You mean—" said Veronica.

"I mean," I said, "that the writer of books is, generally speaking, an exceptionally moral man. That is what leads him astray: he is too good. This world does not come up to his ideas. It is not the world as he would have made it himself. To satisfy his craving for morality he sets to work to make a world of his own. It is not this world. It is not a bit like this world. In a world as it should be, Veronica, you would undoubtedly have been blown up—if not altogether, at all events partially. What you have to do, Veronica, is, with a full heart, to praise Heaven that this is not a perfect world. If it were I doubt very much, Veronica, your being here. That you are here happy and thriving proves that all is not as it should be. The bull of this world, feeling he wants to toss somebody, does not sit upon himself, so to speak, till the wicked child comes by. He takes the first child that turns up, and thanks God for it. A hundred to one it is the best child for miles around. The bull does not care. He spoils that pattern child. He'd spoil a bishop, feeling as he does that morning. Your little friend in the velvet suit who did get himself blown up, at all events as regards the suit—Which of you was it that thought of that gunpowder, you or he?"

Veronica claimed that the inspiration had been hers.

"I can easily believe it. And was he anxious to steal the gunpowder and put it on the fire, or did he have to be persuaded?"

Veronica admitted that in the qualities of a first-class hero he was wanting. Not till it had been suggested to him that he must at heart be a cowardy cowardy custard had he been moved to take a hand in the enterprise.

"A lad, clearly," I continued, "that left to himself would be a comfort to his friends. And the story of the robbers—your invention or his?"

Veronica was generously of opinion that he might have thought of it had he not been chiefly concerned at the moment with the idea of getting home to his mother. As it was, the clothing with romance of incidents otherwise bald and uninteresting had fallen upon her.

"The good child of the story. The fact stands out at every point. His one failing an amiable weakness. Do you not see it for yourself, Veronica? In the book, you, not he, would have tumbled over the mat. In this wicked world it is the wicked who prosper. He, the innocent, the virtuous, is torn into rags. You, the villain of the story, escape."

"I see," said Veronica; "then whenever nothing happens to you that means that you're a wrong 'un."

"I don't go so far as to say that, Veronica. And I wish you wouldn't use slang. Dick is a man, and a man—well, never mind about a man. You, Veronica, must never forget that you're a lady. Justice must not be looked for in this world. Sometimes the wicked get what they deserve. More often they don't. There seems to be no rule. Follow the dictates of your conscience, Veronica, and blow—I mean be indifferent to the consequences. Sometimes you'll come out all right, and sometimes you won't. But the beautiful sensation will always be with you: I did right. Things have turned out unfortunately: but that's not my fault. Nobody can blame me."

"But they do," said Veronica, "they blame you just as if you'd meant to go and do it."

"It does not matter, Veronica," I pointed out, "the opinion of the world. The good man disregards it."

"But they send you to bed," persisted Veronica.

"Let them," I said. "What is bed so long as the voice of the inward Monitor consoles us with the reflection—"

"But it don't," interrupted Veronica; "it makes you feel all the madder. It does really."

"It oughtn't to," I told her.

"Then why does it?" argued Veronica. "Why don't it do what it ought to?"

The trouble about arguing with children is that they will argue too.

"Life's a difficult problem, Veronica," I allowed. "Things are not as they ought to be, I admit it. But one must not despair. Something's got to be done."

"It's jolly hard on some of us," said Veronica. "Strive as you may, you can't please everyone. And if you just as much as stand up for yourself, oh, crikey!"

"The duty of the grown-up person, Veronica," I said, "is to bring up the child in the way that it should go. It isn't easy work, and occasionally irritability may creep in."

"There's such a lot of 'em at it," grumbled Veronica. "There are times, between 'em all, when you don't know whether you're standing on your head or your heels."

"They mean well, Veronica," I said. "When I was a little boy I used to think just as you do. But now—"

"Did you ever get into rows?" interrupted Veronica.

"Did I ever?—was never out of them, so far as I can recollect. If it wasn't one thing, then it was another."

"And didn't it make you wild?" enquired Veronica, "when first of all they'd ask what you'd got to say and why you'd done it, and then, when you tried to explain things to them, wouldn't listen to you?"

"What used to irritate me most, Veronica," I replied—"I can remember it so well—was when they talked steadily for half an hour themselves, and then, when I would attempt with one sentence to put them right about the thing, turn round and bully-rag me for being argumentative."

"If they would only listen," agreed Veronica, "you might get them to grasp things. But no, they talk and talk, till at the end they don't know what they are talking about themselves, and then they pretend it's your fault for having made them tired."

"I know," I said, "they always end up like that. 'I am tired of talking to you,' they say—as if we were not tired of listening to them!"

"And then when you think," said Veronica, "they say you oughtn't to think. And if you don't think, and let it out by accident, then they say 'why don't you think?' It don't seem as though we could do right. It makes one almost despair."

"And it isn't even as if they were always right themselves," I pointed out to her. "When they knock over a glass it is, 'Who put that glass there?' You'd think that somebody had put it there on purpose and made it invisible. They are not expected to see a glass six inches in front of their nose, in the place where the glass ought to be. The way they talk you'd suppose that a glass had no business on a table. If I broke it, then it was always, 'Clumsy little devil! ought to have his dinner in the nursery.' If they mislay their things and can't find them, it's, 'Who's been interfering with my things? Who's been in here rummaging about?' Then when they find it they want to know indignantly who put it there. If I could not find a thing, for the simple reason that somebody had taken it away and put it somewhere else, then wherever they had put it was the right place for it, and I was a little idiot for not knowing it."

"And of course you mustn't say anything," commented Veronica. "Oh, no! If they do something silly and you just point it out to them, then there is always a reason for it that you wouldn't understand. Oh, yes! And if you make just the slightest mistake, like what is natural to all of us, that is because you are wicked and unfeeling and don't want to be anything else."

"I will tell you what we will do, Veronica," I said; "we will write a book. You shall help me. And in it the children shall be the wise and good people who never make mistakes, and they shall boss the show— you know what I mean—look after the grown-up people and bring them up properly. And everything the grown-up people do, or don't do, will be wrong."

Veronica clapped her hands. "No, will you really?" she said. "Oh, do."

"I will really," I answered. "We will call it a moral tale for parents; and all the children will buy it and give it to their fathers and mothers and such-like folk for their birthdays, with writing on the title-page, 'From Johnny, or Jenny, to dear Papa, or to dear Aunty, with every good wish for his or her improvement!'"

"Do you think they will read it?" doubted Veronica.

"We will put in it something shocking," I suggested, "and get some paper to denounce it as a disgrace to English literature. And if that won't do it we will say it is a translation from the Russian. The children shall stop at home and arrange what to have for dinner, and the grown-up people shall be sent to school. We will start them off each morning with a little satchel. They shall be made to read 'Grimm's Fairy Tales' in the original German, with notes; and learn 'Old Mother Hubbard' by heart and explain the grammar."

"And go to bed early," suggested Veronica.

"We will have them all in bed by eight o'clock, Veronica, and they will go cheerfully, as if they liked it, or we will know the reason why. We will make them say their prayers. Between ourselves, Veronica, I don't believe they always do. And no reading in bed, and no final glass of whisky toddy, or any nonsense of that sort. An Abernethy biscuit and perhaps if they are good a jujube, and then 'Good night,' and down with their head on the pillow. And no calling out, and no pretending they have got a pain in their tummy and creeping downstairs in their night-shirts and clamouring for brandy. We will be up to all their tricks."

"And they'll have to take their medicine," Veronica remembered.

"The slightest suggestion of sulkiness, the first intimation that they are not enjoying themselves, will mean cod liver oil in a tablespoon, Veronica."

"And we will ask them why they never use their commonsense," chirped Veronica.

"That will be our trouble, Veronica; that they won't have any sense of any sort—not what we shall deem sense. But, nevertheless, we will be just. We will always give them a reason why they have got to do everything they don't want to do, and nothing that they want to do. They won't understand it and they won't agree that it is a reason; but they will keep that to themselves, if they are wise."

"And of course they must not argue," Veronica insisted.

"If they answer back, Veronica, that will show they are cursed with an argumentative temperament which must be rooted out at any cost,"

I agreed; "and if they don't say anything, that will prove them possessed of a surly disposition which must be checked at once, before it develops into a vice."

"And whatever we do to them we will tell them it's for their own good," Veronica chortled.

"Of course it will be for their own good," I answered. "That will be our chief pleasure—making them good and happy. It won't be their pleasure, but that will be owing to their ignorance."

"They will be grateful to us later on," gurgled Veronica.

"With that assurance we will comfort them from time to time," I answered. "We will be good to them in all ways. We will let them play games—not stupid games, golf and croquet, that do you no good and lead only to language and dispute—but bears and wolves and whales; educational sort of games that will aid them in acquiring knowledge of natural history. We will show them how to play Pirates and Red Indians and Ogres—sensible play that will help them to develop their imaginative faculties. That is why grown-up people are so dull; they are never made to think. But now and then," I continued, "we will let them play their own games, say on Wednesday and Saturday afternoons. We will invite other grown-ups to come to tea with them, and let them flirt in the garden, or if wet make love in the dining-room, till nurse comes for them. But we, of course, must choose their friends for them—nice, well-behaved ladies and gentlemen, the parents of respectable children; because left to themselves—well, you know what they are! They would just as likely fall in love with quite undesirable people—men and women we could not think of having about the house. We will select for them companions we feel sure will be the most suitable for them; and if they don't like them—if Uncle William says he can't bear the girl we have invited up to love him—that he positively hates her, we till tell him that it is only his wilful temper, and that he's got to like her because she's good for him; and don't let us have any of his fretfulness. And if Grandmamma pouts and says she won't love old man Jones merely because he's got a red nose, or a glass eye, or some silly reason of that sort, we will say to her: 'All right, my lady, you will play with Mr. Jones and be nice to him, or you will spend the afternoon putting your room tidy; make up your mind.' We will let them marry (on Wednesday and Saturday afternoons), and play at keeping house. And if they quarrel we will shake them and take the babies away from them, and lock them up in drawers, and tell them they sha'n't have them again till they are good."

"And the more they try to be good, the more it will turn out that they ain't been good," Veronica reflected.

"Their goodness and their badness will depend upon us in more senses than one, Veronica," I explained. "When Consols are down, when the east wind has touched up our liver, they will be surprised how bad they are."

"And they mustn't ever forget what they've ever been once told," crowed Veronica. "We mustn't have to tell 'em the same thing over and over again, like we was talking to brick walls."

"And if we meant to tell them and forgot to tell them," I added, "we will tell them that they ought not to want us to tell them a simple thing like that, as if they were mere babies. We must remember all these points."

"And if they grumble we'll tell them that's 'cos they don't know how happy they are. And we'll tell them how good we used to be when—I say, don't you miss your train, or I shall get into a row."

"Great Scott! I'd forgotten all about that train, Veronica," I admitted.

"Better run," suggested Veronica.

It sounded good advice.

"Keep on thinking about that book," shouted Veronica.

"Make a note of things as they occur to you," I shouted back.

"What shall we call it?" Veronica screamed.

"'Why the Man in the Moon looks sat upon,'" I shrieked.

When I turned again she was sitting on the top rail of the stile conducting an imaginary orchestra with one of her own shoes. The six-fifteen was fortunately twenty minutes late.

I THOUGHT IT BEST TO tell Ethelbertha the truth; that things had gone wrong with the kitchen stove.

"Let me know the worst," she said. "Is Veronica hurt?"

"The worst," I said, "is that I shall have to pay for a new range. Why, when anything goes amiss, poor Veronica should be assumed as a matter of course to be in it, appears to me unjust."

"You are sure she's all right?" persisted Ethelbertha.

"Honest Injun—confound those children and their slang—I mean positively," I answered. The Little Mother looked relieved.

I told her all the trouble we had had in connection with the cow. Her sympathies were chiefly with the cow. I told her I had hopes of Robina's developing into a sensible woman. We talked quite a deal about Robina.

We agreed that between us we had accomplished something rather clever.

"I must get back as soon as I can," I said. "I don't want young Bute getting wrong ideas into his head."

"Who is young Bute?" she asked.

"The architect," I explained.

"I thought he was an old man," said Ethelbertha.

"Old Spreight is old enough," I said. "Young Bute is one of his young men; but he understands his work, and seems intelligent."

"What's he like?" she asked.

"Personally, an exceedingly nice young fellow. There's a good deal of sense in him. I like a boy who listens."

"Good-looking?" she asked.

"Not objectionably so," I replied. "A pleasant face—particularly when he smiles."

"Is he married?" she asked.

"Really, it did not occur to me to ask him," I admitted. "How curious you women are! No, I don't think so. I should say not."

"Why don't you think so?" she demanded.

"Oh, I don't know. He doesn't give you the idea of a married man. You'll like him. Seems so fond of his sister."

"Shall we be seeing much of him?" she asked.

"A goodish deal," I answered. "I expect he will be going down on Monday. Very annoying, this stove business."

"What is the use of his being there without you?" Ethelbertha wanted to know.

"Oh, he'll potter round," I suggested, "and take measurements. Dick will be about to explain things to him. Or, if he isn't, there's Robina—awkward thing is, Robina seems to have taken a dislike to him."

"Why has she taken a dislike to him?" asked Ethelbertha.

"Oh, because he mistook the back of the house for the front, or the front of the house for the back," I explained; "I forget which now. Says it's his smile that irritates her. She owns herself there's no real reason."

"When will you be going down again?" Ethelbertha asked.

"On Thursday next," I told her; "stove or no stove."

She said she would come with me. She felt the change would do her good, and promised not to do anything when she got there. And then I told her all that I had done for Dick.

"The ordinary farmer," I pointed out to her, "is so often a haphazard type of man with no ideas. If successful, it is by reason of a natural instinct which cannot be taught. St. Leonard has studied the theory of the thing. From him Dick will learn all that can be learnt about farming. The selection, I felt, demanded careful judgment."

"But will Dick stick to it?" Ethelbertha wondered.

"There, again," I pointed out to her, "the choice was one calling for exceptional foresight. The old man—as a matter of fact, he isn't old at all; can't be very much older than myself; I don't know why they all call him the old man—has formed a high opinion of Dick. His daughter told me so, and I have taken care to let Dick know it. The boy will not care to disappoint him. Her mother—"

"Whose mother?" interrupted Ethelbertha.

"Janie's mother, Mrs. St. Leonard," I explained. "She also has formed a good opinion of him. The children like him. Janie told me so."

"She seems to do a goodish deal of talking, this Miss Janie," remarked Ethelbertha.

"You will like her," I said. "She is a charming girl—so sensible, and good, and unselfish, and—"

"Who told you all this about her?" interrupted Ethelbertha.

"You can see it for yourself," I answered. "The mother appears to be a nonentity, and St. Leonard himself—well, he is not a business man. It is Janie who manages everything—keeps everything going."

"What is she like?" asked Ethelbertha.

"I am telling you," I said. "She is so practical, and yet at the same time—"

"In appearance, I mean," explained Ethelbertha.

"How you women," I said, "do worry about mere looks! What does it matter? If you want to know, it is that sort of face that grows upon you. At first you do not notice how beautiful it is, but when you come to look into it—"

"And has she also formed a high opinion of Dick?" interrupted Ethelbertha.

"She will be disappointed in him," I said, "if he does not work hard and stick to it. They will all be disappointed in him."

"What's it got to do with them?" demanded Ethelbertha.

"I'm not thinking about them," I said. "What I look at is—"

"I don't like her," said Ethelbertha. "I don't like any of them."

"But—" She didn't seem to be listening.

"I know that class of man," she said; "and the wife appears, if anything, to be worse. As for the girl—"

"When you come to know them—" I said.

She said she didn't want to know them. She wanted to go down on Monday, early.

I got her to see—it took some little time—the disadvantages of this. We should only be adding to Robina's troubles; and change of plan now would unsettle Dick's mind.

"He has promised to write me," I said, "and tell me the result of his first day's experience. Let us wait and hear what he says."

She said that whatever could have possessed her to let me take those poor unfortunate children away from her, and muddle up everything without her, was a mystery to herself. She hoped that, at least, I had done nothing irrevocable in the case of Veronica.

"Veronica," I said, "is really wishful, I think, to improve. I have bought her a donkey."

"A what?" exclaimed Ethelbertha.

"A donkey," I repeated. "The child took a fancy to it, and we all agreed it might help to steady her—give her a sense of responsibility."

"I somehow felt you hadn't overlooked Veronica," said Ethelbertha.

I thought it best to change the conversation. She seemed in a fretful mood.

VIII

R obina's letter was dated Monday evening, and reached us Tuesday morning.

"I HOPE YOU CAUGHT YOUR train," she wrote. "Veronica did not get back till half-past six. She informed me that you and she had found a good deal to talk about, and that 'one thing had led to another.' She is a quaint young imp, but I think your lecture must have done her good. Her present attitude is that of gentle forbearance to all around her—not without its dignity. She has not snorted once, and at times is really helpful. I have given her an empty scribbling diary we found in your desk, and most of her spare time she remains shut up with it in the bedroom. She tells me you and she are writing a book together. I asked her what about. She waved me aside with the assurance that I would know 'all in good time,' and that it was going to do good. I caught sight of just the title-page last night. It was lying open on the dressing-table: 'Why the Man in the Moon looks sat upon.' It sounds like a title of yours. But I would not look further, though tempted. She has drawn a picture underneath. It is really not bad. The old gentleman really does look sat upon, and intensely disgusted.

"'Sir Robert'—his name being Theodore, which doesn't seem to suit him—turns out to be the only son of a widow, a Mrs. Foy, our next-door neighbour to the south. We met her coming out of church on Sunday morning. She was still crying. Dick took Veronica on ahead, and I walked part of the way home with them. Her grandfather, it appears, was killed many years ago by the bursting of a boiler; and she is haunted, poor lady, by the conviction that Theodore is the inheritor of an hereditary tendency to getting himself blown up. She attaches no blame to us, seeing in Saturday's catastrophe only the hand of the Family Curse. I tried to comfort her with the idea that the Curse having spent itself upon a futile effort, nothing further need now be feared from it; but she persists in taking the gloomier view that in wrecking our kitchen, Theodore's 'Doom,' as she calls it, was merely indulging in a sort of dress rehearsal; the finishing performance may be relied upon to follow. It sounds ridiculous, but the poor woman was so desperately in earnest that when an unlucky urchin, coming out of a cottage we were passing, tripped on the doorstep and let fall a jug, we both screamed at the same time, and were equally surprised to find 'Sir Robert' still between us and all in one piece. I thought it foolish to discuss all this before the child himself; but did not like to stop her. As a result, he regards himself evidently as the chosen foe of Heaven, and is not, unnaturally, proud of himself. She called here this (Monday) afternoon to leave cards; and, at her request, I showed her the kitchen and the mat over which he had stumbled. She seemed surprised that the 'Doom' had let slip so favourable a chance of accomplishing its business, and gathered from the fact added cause for anxiety. Evidently something much more thorough is in store for Master Theodore. It was only half a pound of gunpowder, she told me. Doctor Smallboy's gardener had bought it for the purpose of raising the stump of an old elm-tree, and had left it for a moment on the grass while he had returned to the house for more brown paper. She seemed pleased with the gardener, who, as she said, might, if dishonestly inclined, have charged her for a pound. I wanted to pay for—at all events—our share, but she would not take a penny. Her late lamented grandfather she regards as the person responsible for the entire incident, and perhaps it may be as well not to disturb her view. Had I suggested it, I feel sure she would have seen the justice of her providing us with a new kitchen range.

"Wildly exaggerated accounts of the affair are flying round the neighbourhood; and my chief fear is that Veronica may discover she is a local celebrity. Your sudden disappearance is supposed to have been heavenward. An old farm labourer who saw you pass on your way to the station speaks of you as 'the ghost of the poor gentleman himself;' and fragments of clothing found anywhere within a radius of two miles are being preserved, I am told, as specimens of your remains. Boots would appear to have been your chief apparel. Seven pairs have already been collected from the surrounding ditches. Among the more public-spirited there is talk of using you to start a local museum."

THESE FIRST THREE PARAGRAPHS I did not read to Ethelbertha. Fortunately they just filled the first sheet, which I took an opportunity of slipping into my pocket unobserved.

"THE NEW BOY ARRIVED ON Sunday morning," she continued. "His name—if I have got it right—is William. Anyhow, that is the nearest I can get to it. His other name, if any, I must leave you to extract from him yourself. It may be Berkshire that he talks, but it sounds more like barking. Please excuse the pun; but I have just been talking to him for half an hour, trying to make him understand that I want him to go home, and maybe, as a result, I am feeling a little hysterical. Anything more rural I cannot imagine. But he is anxious to learn, and a fairly wide field is in front of him. I caught him after our breakfast on Sunday calmly throwing everything left over onto the dust-heap. I pointed out to him the wickedness of wasting nourishing food, and impressed upon him that the proper place for victuals was inside us. He never answers. He stands stock still, with his mouth as wide open as it will go—which is saying a good deal—and one trusts that one's words are entering into him. All Sunday afternoon he was struggling valiantly against an almost supernatural sleepiness. After tea he got worse, and I began to think he would be no use to me. We none of us ate much supper; and Dick, who appears able to understand him, helped him to carry the things out. I heard them talking, and then Dick came back and closed the door behind him. 'He wants to know,' said Dick, 'if he can leave the corned beef over till to-morrow. Because, if he eats it all to-night, he doesn't think he will be able to walk home.'

"Veronica takes great interest in him. She has evidently a motherly side to her character, for which we none of us have given her credit. She says she is sure there is good in him. She sits beside him while he chops wood, and tells him carefully selected stories, calculated, she argues, to develop his intelligence. She is careful, moreover, not to hurt his feelings by any display of superiority. 'Of course, anyone leading a useful life, such as yours,' I overheard her saying to him this morning, 'don't naturally get much time for reading. I've nothing else to do, you see, 'cept to improve myself.'

"The donkey arrived this afternoon while I was out—galloping, I am given to understand, with 'Opkins on his back. There seems to be some secret between those two. We have tried him with hay, and we have tried him with thistles; but he seems to prefer bread-and-butter. I have not been able as yet to find out whether he takes tea or coffee in the morning. But he is an animal that evidently knows his own mind, and fortunately both are in the house. We are putting him up for to-night with the cow, who greeted him at first with enthusiasm and wanted to adopt him, but has grown cold to him since on discovering that he is not a calf. I have been trying to make friends with her, but she is so very unresponsive. She doesn't seem to want anything but grass, and prefers to get that for herself. She doesn't seem to want to be happy ever again.

"A funny thing happened in church. I was forgetting to tell you. The St. Leonards occupy two pews at the opposite end from the door. They were all there when we arrived, with the exception of the old gentleman himself. He came in just before the 'Dearly Beloved,' when everybody was standing up. A running fire of suppressed titters followed him up the aisle, and some of the people laughed outright. I could see no reason why. He looked a dignified old gentleman in his grey hair and tightly buttoned frock coat, which gives him a somewhat military appearance. But when he came level with our pew I understood. Hurrying back from his morning round, and with no one there to superintend him, the dear old absent-minded thing had forgotten to change his breeches. From a little above the knee upward he was a perfect Christian; but his legs were just those of a disreputable sinner.

"'What's the joke?' he whispered to me as he passed—I was in the corner seat. 'Have I missed it?'

"We called round on them after lunch, and at once I was appealed to for my decision.

"'Now, here's a plain sensible girl,' exclaimed the old gentleman the moment I entered the room.' (You will notice I put no comma after 'plain.' I am taking it he did not intend one. You can employ one adjective to qualify another, can't you?) 'And I will put it to her, What difference can it make to the Almighty whether I go to church in trousers or in breeches?'

"'I do not see,' retorted Mrs. St. Leonard somewhat coldly, 'that Miss Robina is in any better position than myself to speak with authority on the views of the Almighty'—which I felt was true. 'If it makes no difference to the Almighty, then why not, for my sake, trousers?'

"'The essential thing,' he persisted, 'is a contrite heart.' He was getting very cross.

"'It may just as well be dressed respectably,' was his wife's opinion. He left the room, slamming the door.

"I do like Janie the more and more I see of her. I do hope she will let me get real chums with her. She does me so much good. (I read that bit twice over to Ethelbertha, pretending I had lost the place.) I suppose it is having rather a silly mother and an unpractical father that has made her so capable. If you and Little Mother had been proper sort of parents I might have been quite a decent sort of girl. But it's too late finding fault with you now. I suppose I must put up with you. She works so hard, and is so unselfish. But she is not like some good people, who make you feel it is hopeless your trying to be good. She gets cross and impatient; and then she laughs at herself, and gets right again that way. Poor Mrs. St. Leonard! I cannot help feeling sorry for her. She would have been so happy as the wife of a really respectable City man, who would have gone off every morning with a flower in his buttonhole and have worn a white waistcoat on Sundays. I don't believe what they say: that husbands and wives should be the opposite of one another. Mr. St. Leonard ought to have married a brainy woman, who would have discussed philosophy with him, and have been just as happy drinking beer out of a tea-cup: you know the sort I mean. If ever I marry it will be a short-tempered man who loves music and is a good dancer; and if I find out too late that he's clever I'll run away from him.

"Dick has not yet come home—nearly eight o'clock. Veronica is supposed to be in bed, but I can hear things falling. Poor boy! I expect he'll be tired; but to-day is an exception. Three hundred sheep have had to be brought all the way from Ilsley, and must be 'herded'—I fancy it is called—before anybody can think of supper. I saw to it that he had a good dinner.

"And now to come to business. Young Bute has been here all day, and has only just left. He is coming down again on Friday—which, by the way, don't forget is Mrs. St. Leonard's 'At Home' day. She hopes she may then have the pleasure of making your acquaintance, and thinks that possibly there may be present one or two people we may like to know. From which I gather that half the neighbourhood has been specially invited to meet you. So mind you bring a frock-coat; and if Little Mother can put her hand easily on my pink muslin with the spots—it is either in my wardrobe or else in the bottom drawer in Veronica's room, if it isn't in the cardboard box underneath mother's bed—you might slip it into your bag. But whatever you do don't crush it. The sash I feel sure mother put away somewhere herself. He sees no reason—I'm talking now about young Bute,—if you approve his plans, why work should not be commenced immediately. Shall I write old Slee to meet you at the house on Friday? From all accounts I don't think you'll do better. He is on the spot, and they say he is most reasonable. But you have to get estimates, don't you? He suggests—Mr. Bute, I mean—throwing what used to be the dairy into the passage, which will make a hall big enough for anything. We might even give a dance in it, he thinks. But all this you will be able to discuss with him on Friday. He has evidently taken a great deal of pains, and some of his suggestions sound sensible. But of course he must fully understand that it is what we want, not what he thinks, that is important. I told him you said I could have my room exactly as I liked it myself; and I have explained to him my ideas. He seemed at first to be under the impression that I didn't know what I was talking about, so I made it quite clear to him that I did, with the result that he has consented to carry out my instructions, on condition that I put them down in black and white—which I think just as well, as then there can be no excuse afterwards for argument. I like him better than I did the first time. About everything else he can be fairly amiable. It is when he talks about 'frontal elevations' and 'ground plans' that he irritates me. Tell Little Mother that I'll write her to-morrow. Couldn't she come down with you on Friday? Everything will be ship-shape by then; and—"

The remainder was of a nature more private. She concluded with a postscript, which also I did not read to Ethelbertha.

"Thought I had finished telling you everything, when quite a stylish rat-tat sounded on the door. I placed an old straw hat of Dick's in a prominent position, called loudly to an imaginary 'John' not to go without the letters, and then opened it. He turned out to be the local reporter. I need not have been alarmed. He was much the more nervous of the two, and was so full of excuses that had I not come to his rescue I believe he would have gone away forgetting what he'd come for. Nothing save an overwhelming sense of duty to the Public (with a capital P) could have induced him to inflict himself upon me. Could I give him a few details which would enable him to set rumour right? I immediately saw visions of headlines: 'Domestic Tragedy!' 'Eminent Author blown up by his own Daughter!' 'Once Happy Home now a Mere Wreck!' It seemed to me our only plan was to enlist this amiable young man upon our side; I hope I did not overdo it. My idea was to convey the impression that one glance at him had convinced me he was the best and noblest of mankind; that I felt I could rely upon his wit and courage to save us from a notoriety that, so far as I was concerned, would sadden my whole life; and that if he did so eternal gratitude and admiration would be the least I could lay at his feet. I can be nice when I try. People have said so. We parted with only a pressure of the hand, and I hope he won't get into trouble, but I see *The Berkshire Courier* is going to be deprived of its prey. Dick has just come in. He promises to talk when he has finished eating."

Dick's letter, for which Ethelbertha seemed to be strangely impatient, reached us on Wednesday morning.

"If ever you want to find out, Dad, what hard work really means, you try farming," wrote Dick; "and yet I believe you would like it. Hasn't some old Johnny somewhere described it as the poetry of the ploughshare? Why did we ever take to bothering about anything else—shutting ourselves up in stuffy offices, worrying ourselves to death about a lot of rubbish that isn't any good to anybody? I wish I could put it properly, Dad; you would see just what I mean. Why don't we live in simply-built houses and get most everything we want out of the land: which we easily could? You take a dozen poor devils away from walking behind the plough and put them down into coal-mines, and set them running about half-naked among a lot of roaring furnaces, and between them they turn out a machine that does the ploughing for them. What is the sense of it? Of course some things are useful. I would like a motor-car, and railways and steamboats are all right; but it seems to me that half the fiddle-faddles we fancy we want we'd be just as well, if not better, without, and there would be all that time and energy to spare for the sort of things that everybody ought to have. It's everywhere just like it was at school. They kept us so hard at it, studying Greek roots, we hadn't time to learn English grammar. Look at young Dennis Yewbury. He's got two thousand acres up in Scotland. He could lead a jolly life turning the place into some real use. Instead of which he lets it all run to waste for nothing but to breed a few hundred birds that wouldn't keep a single family alive; while he works from morning till night at humbugging people in a beastly hole in the City, just to fill his house with a host of silly gim-cracks and dress up himself and his women-folk like peacocks. Of course we would always want clever chaps like you to tell us stories; and doctors we couldn't do without, though I guess if we were leading sensible lives we'd be able to get along with about half of them. It seems to me that what we want is a comfortable home, enough to eat and drink, and a few fal-lal sort of things to make the girls look pretty; and that all the rest is rot. We would all of us have time then to think and play a bit, and if we were all working fairly at something really useful and were contented with our own share, there'd be enough for everybody.

"I suppose this is all nonsense, but I wish it wasn't. Anyway, it's what I mean to do myself; and I'm awfully much obliged to you, Dad, for giving me this chance. You've hit the right nail on the head this time.

Farming was what I was meant for; I feel it. I would have hated being a barrister, setting people by the ears and making my living out of other people's troubles. Being a farmer you feel that in doing good to yourself you are doing good all round. Miss Janie agrees with all I say. I think she is one of the most sensible girls I have ever come across, and Robin likes her awfully. So is the old man: he's a brick. I think he has taken a liking to me, and I know I have to him. He's the dearest old fellow imaginable. The very turnips he seems to think of as though they were so many rows of little children. And he makes you see the inside of things. Take fields now, for instance. I used to think a field was just a field. You scraped it about and planted it with seeds, and everything else depended on the weather. Why, Dad, it's alive! There are good fields that want to get on—that are grateful for everything you do for them, and take a pride in themselves. And there are brutes of fields that you feel you want to kick. You can waste a hundred pounds' worth of manure on them, and it only makes them more stupid than they were before. One of our fields—a wizened-looking eleven-acre strip bordering the Fyfield road—he has christened Mrs. Gummidge: it seems to feel everything more than any other field. From whatever point of the compass the wind blows that field gets the most harm from it. You would think to look at it after a storm that there hadn't been any rain in any other field—that that particular field must have got it all; while two days' sunshine has the effect upon it that a six weeks' drought would on any other field. His theory (he must have a theory to account for everything; it comforts him. He has just hit upon a theory that explains why twins are born with twice as much original sin as other children, and doesn't seem to mind now what they do) is that each odd corner of the earth has gained a character of its own from the spirits of the countless dead men buried in its bosom. 'Robbers and thieves,' he will say, kicking the sod of some field all stones and thistles; 'silly fighting men who thought God built the world merely to give them the fun of knocking it about. Look at them, the fools! stones and thistles—thistles and stones: that is their notion of a field.' Or, leaning over the gate of some field of rich-smelling soil, he will stretch out his arms as though to caress it: 'Brave lads!' he will say; 'kindly honest fellows who loved the poor peasant folk.' I fancy he has not got much sense of humour; or if he has, it is a humour he leaves you to find out for yourself. One does not feel one wants to laugh, listening even to his most whimsical ideas; and anyhow it is a fact that of two fields quite close to one another, one will be worth ten pounds an acre and the other dear at half a crown, and there seems to be nothing to explain it. We have a seven-acre patch just halfway up the hill. He says he never passes it without taking off his hat to it. Whatever you put in it does well; while other fields, try them with what you will, it is always the very thing they did not want. You might fancy them fractious children, always crying for the other child's bun. There is really no reason for its being such a good field, except its own pluck. It faces the east, and the wood for half the day hides it from the sun; but it makes the best of everything, and even on the greyest day it seems to be smiling at you. 'Some happy-hearted Mother Thing—a singer of love songs the while she toiled,' he will have it, must lie sleeping there. By-the-bye, what a jolly field Janie would make! Don't you think so, Dad?

"What the dickens, Dad, have you done to Veronica? She wanders about everywhere with an exercise book in her hand, and when you say anything to her, instead of answering you back, she sits plump down wherever she is and writes for all she's worth. She won't say what she's up to. She says it's a private matter between you and her, and that later on things are going to be seen in their true light. I told her this morning what I thought of her for forgetting to feed the donkey. I was prepared, of course, for a hundred explanations: First, that she had meant to feed the donkey; secondly, that it wasn't her place to feed the donkey; thirdly, that the donkey would have been fed if circumstances over which she had no control had not arisen rendering it impossible for her to feed the donkey; fourthly, that the morning wasn't the proper time to feed the donkey, and so on. Instead of which, out she whips this ridiculous book and asks me if I would mind saying it over again.

"I keep forgetting to ask Janie what it is he has been accustomed to. We have tried him with thistles, and we've tried him with hay. The thistles he scratches himself against; but for the hay he appears to have no use whatever. Robin thinks his idea is to save us trouble. We are not to get in anything especially for him—whatever we may happen to be having ourselves he will put up with. Bread-and-butter cut thick, or a slice of cake with an apple seems to be his notion of a light lunch; and for drink he fancies tea out of a slop-basin, with two knobs of sugar and plenty of milk. Robin says it's waste of time taking his meals out to him. She says she is going to train him to come in when he hears the gong. We use the alarm clock at present for a gong. I don't know what I shall do when the cow goes away. She wakes me every morning punctually at half-past four, but I'm in a blue funk that one of these days she will oversleep herself. It is one of those clocks you read about. You wrote something rather funny about one once yourself, but I always thought you had invented it. I bought it because they said it was an extra loud one, and so it is. The thing that's wrong about it is that, do what you will, you can't get it to go off before six o'clock in the morning. I set it on Sunday evening for half-past four—we farmers do have to work, I can tell you. But it's worth it. I had no idea that the world was so beautiful. There is a light you never see at any other time, and the whole air seems to be full of fluttering song. You feel—but you must get up and come out with me, Dad. I can't describe it. If it hadn't been for the good old cow, Lord knows what time I'd have been up. The clock went off at half-past four in the afternoon, just as they were sitting down to tea, and frightened them all out of their skins. We have fiddled about with it all we know, but there's no getting it to do anything between six p.m. and six am. Anything you want of it in the daytime it is quite agreeable to. But it seems to have fixed its own working hours, and isn't going to be bustled out of its proper rest. I got so mad with it myself I wanted to pitch it out of the window, but Robin thought we ought to keep it till you came, that perhaps you might be able to do something with it—writing something about it, she means. I said I thought alarm clocks were pretty well played out by this time; but, as she says, there is always a new generation coming along to whom almost everything must be fresh. Anyhow, the confounded thing cost seven and six, and seems to be no good for anything else.

"Whatever was it that you really did say to Robin about her room? Young Bute came round to me on Monday quite upset about it. He says it is going to be all windows, and will look, when finished, like an incorrect copy of the Eddystone lighthouse. He says there will be no place for the bed, and if there is to be a fireplace at all it will have to be in the cupboard, and that the only way, so far as he can see, of her getting in and out of it will be by a door through the bathroom. She said that you said she could have it entirely to her own idea, and that he was just to carry out her instructions; but, as he points out, you can't have a room in a house as if the rest of the house wasn't there, even if it is your own room. Nobody, it seems, will be able to have a bath without first talking it over with her, and arranging a time mutually convenient. I told him I was sure you never meant him to do anything absurd; and that his best plan would be to go straight back to her, explain to her that she'd been talking like a silly goat—he could have put it politely, of course—and that he wasn't going to pay any attention to her. You might have thought I had suggested his walking into a den of lions and pulling all their tails. I don't know what Robin has done to him, but he seems quite frightened of her. I had to promise that I would talk to her. He'd better have done it himself. I only told her just what he said, and off she went in one of her tantrums. You know her style: If she liked to live in a room where she could see to do her hair that was no business of his, and if he couldn't design a plain, simple bedroom that wasn't going to look ridiculous and make her the laughing-stock of all the neighbourhood, then the Royal Institute of British Architects must have strange notions of the sort of person entitled to go about the country building houses; that if he thought the proper place for a fire was in a cupboard, she didn't; that his duty was to carry out the instructions of his employers, and if he imagined for a moment she was going to consent to remain shut up in her room till everybody in the house had finished bathing it would be better for us to secure the services of somebody possessed of a little commonsense; that next time she met him she would certainly tell him what she thought of him, also that she should certainly decline to hold any further communication with him again; that she doesn't want a bedroom now of any sort—perhaps she may be permitted a shakedown in the pantry, or perhaps Veronica will allow her an occasional night's rest with her, and if not it doesn't matter. You'll have to talk to her yourself. I'm not going to say any more.

"Don't forget that Friday is the St. Leonards' 'At Home' day. I've promised Janie that you shall be there in all your best clothes. (Don't tell her I'm calling her Janie. It might offend her. But nobody calls her Miss St. Leonard.) Everybody is coming, and all the children are having their hair washed. You will have it all your own way down here. There's no other celebrity till you get to Boss Croker, the Tammany man, the other side of Ilsley Downs. Artists they don't count. The rumour was all round the place last week that you were here incognito in the person of a dismal-looking Johnny, staying at the 'Fisherman's Retreat,' who used to sit all day in a punt up the backwater drinking whisky. It made me rather mad when I saw him. I suppose it was the whisky that suggested the idea to them. They have got the notion in these parts that a literary man is a sort of inspired tramp. A Mrs. Jaggerswade—or some such name—whom I met here on Sunday and who is coming on Friday, took me aside and asked me 'what sort of things' you said when you talked? She said she felt sure it would be so clever, and, herself, she was looking forward to it; but would I—'quite between ourselves'—advise her to bring the children.

"I say, you will have to talk seriously to Veronica. Country life seems to agree with her. She's taken to poaching already—she and the twins. It was the one sin that hitherto they had never committed, and I fancy the old man was feeling proud of this. Luckily I caught them coming home—with ten dead rabbits strung on a pole, the twins carrying it between them on their shoulders, suggesting the picture of the spies returning from the promised land with that bunch of grapes—Veronica scouting on ahead with, every ten yards, her ear to the ground, listening for hostile footsteps. The thing that troubled her most was that she hadn't heard me coming; she seemed to fear that something had gone wrong with the laws of Nature. They had found the whole collection hanging from a tree, and had persuaded themselves that Providence must have been expecting them. I insisted on their going back with me and showing me the tree, much to their disgust. And fortunately the keeper wasn't about—they are men that love making a row. I talked some fine moral sentiment to her. But she says you have told her that it doesn't matter whether you are good or bad, things happen to you just the same; and this being so she feels she may as well enjoy herself. I asked her why she never seemed able to enjoy herself being good—I believe if I'd always had a kid to bring up I'd have been a model chap myself by this time. Her answer was that she supposed she was born bad. I pointed out to her that was a reflection on you and Little Mother; and she answered she guessed she must be a 'throw-back.' Old Slee's got a dog that ought to have been a fox-terrier, but isn't, and he seems to have been explaining things to her.

"A thing that will trouble you down here, Dad, is the cruelty of the country. They catch these poor little wretches in traps, leaving them sometimes for days suffering what must be to them nothing short of agony—to say nothing of the terror and the hunger. I tried putting my finger in one of the beastly things and keeping it there for just two minutes by my watch. It seemed like twenty. The pain grows more intense with every second, and I'm not a soft, as you know. I've lain half an hour with a broken leg, and that wasn't as bad. One hears the little creatures screaming, but cannot find them. Of course when one draws near they keep silent. It makes one quite dislike country people. They are so callous. When you speak to them about it they only grin. Janie goes nearly mad about it. Mr. St. Leonard tried to get the clergyman to say something on the subject, but he answered that he thought it better 'for the Church to confine herself to the accomplishment of her own great mission.' Ass!

"Bring Little Mother down; we want to show her off on Friday. And make her put on something pretty. Ask her if she's got that lilac thing with lace she wore at Cambridge for the May Week the year before last. Tell her not to be silly; it wasn't a bit too young. Nash said she looked like something out of an old picture, and he's going to be an artist. Don't let her dress herself. She doesn't understand it. And will you get me a gun—"

The remainder of the letter was taken up with instructions concerning the gun. It seemed a complicated sort of gun. I wished I hadn't read about the gun to Ethelbertha. It made her nervous for the rest of the day.

Veronica's letter followed on Thursday morning. I read it going down in the train. In transcribing I have thought it better, as regards the spelling, to adopt the more conventional forms.

"You will be pleased to hear," Veronica wrote, "that we are all quite well. Robin works very hard. But I think it does her good. And of course I help her. All I can. I am glad she has got a boy. To do the washing-up. I think that was too much for her. It used to make her cross. One cannot blame her. It is trying work. And it makes you mucky. He is a good boy. But has been neglected. So doesn't know much. I am teaching him grammar. He says 'you was' and 'her be.' But is getting better. He says he went to school. But they couldn't have taken any trouble with him. Could they? The system, I suppose, was rotten. Robina says I mustn't overdo it. Because you want him to talk Berkshire. So I propose confining our attention to the elementary rules. He had never heard of Robinson Crusoe. What a life! We went to church on Sunday. I could not find my gloves. And Robina was waxy. But Mr. St. Leonard came without his trousers. Which was worse. We found them in the evening. The little boy that blew up our stove was there with his mother. But I didn't speak to her. He's got a doom. That's what made him blow it up. He couldn't help it. So you see it wasn't my fault. After all. His grandfather was blown up. And he's going to be blown up again. Later on. But he is very brave. And is going to make a will. I like all the St. Leonards very much. We went there to tea on

Sunday. And Mr. St. Leonard said I was bright. I think Miss Janie very beautiful. And so does Dick. She makes me think of angels. So she does Dick. And he says she is so kind to her little brothers and sisters. It is a good sign. I think she ought to marry Dick. It would steady him. He works very hard. But I think it does him good. We have breakfast at seven. And I lay the table. It is very beautiful in the morning. When you are once up. Mrs. St. Leonard has twins. They are a great anxiety to her. But she would not part from them. She has had much trouble. And is sometimes very sad. I like the girl best. Her name is Winnie. She is more like a boy. His name is Wilfrid. But sometimes they change clothes. Then you're done. They are only nearly seven. But they know a lot. They are going to teach me swimming. Is it not kind of them? The two older boys are at home for their holidays. But they give themselves a lot of airs. And they called me a flapper. I told him he'd be sorry. When he was a man. Because perhaps I'd grow up beautiful. And then he'd fall in love with me. But he said he wouldn't. So I let him see what I thought of him. The little girl is very nice. She is about my own age. Her name is Sally. We are going to write a play. But we sha'n't let Bertie act in it. Unless he turns over a new leaf. I'm going to be a princess that doesn't know it. But only feels it. And she's going to be a wicked witch. What wants me to marry her son. What's a sight. But I won't, because I'd rather die first. And am in love with a swineherd. That is a genius. Only nobody suspects it. I wear a crown in the last act. And everybody rejoices. Except her. I think it will be good. We have nearly finished the first act. She writes very well. And has a sense of atmosphere. And I tell her what to say. Miss Janie is going to make me a dress with a train. And gold spangles. And Robina is going to lend me her blue necklace. Anything will do of course for the old witch. So it won't be much trouble to anyone. Mr. Bute is going to paint us some scenery. And we are going to invite everybody. He is very nice. Robina says he thinks too much of himself. By a long chalk. But she is very critical where men are concerned. She admits it. She says she can't help it. I find him very affable. And so does Dick. We think Robina will get over it. And he has promised not to be angry with her. Because I have told him that she does not mean it. It is only her way. She says she feels it is unjust of her. Because really he is rather charming. I told him that. And he said I was a dear little girl. He is going to get me a real crown. Robina says he has nice eyes. I told him that. And he laughed. There is a gentleman comes here that I think is in love with Robina. But I shouldn't say anything to her about it. If I was you. She is very snappy about it. He is not handsome. But he looks good. He writes for the papers. But I don't think he is rich. And Robina is very nice to him. Until he's gone. Then she gets mad. It all began with the explosion. So perhaps it was fate. He is going to keep it out of the papers. As much as he can. But of course he owes a duty to the public. I am going to decline to see him. I think it better. Mr. Slee says everything will be in apple-pie order to-morrow. So you can come down. And we are going to have Irish stew. And roly-poly pudding. It will be a change. He is very nice. And says he was always in trouble himself when he was a little boy. It's all experience. We are all going on Friday to a party at Mr. St. Leonard's. And you have got to come too. Robina says I can wear my new frock. But we can't find the sash. It is very strange. Because I remember having seen it. You didn't take it for anything, did you? We shall have to get a new one, I suppose. It is very annoying. My new shoes have also not worn well. And they ought to have. Because Robina says they were expensive. The donkey has come. And he is sweet. He eats out of my hand. And lets me kiss him. But he won't go. He goes a little when you shout at him. Very loud. Me and Robina went for a drive yesterday after tea. And Dick ran beside. And shouted. But he got hoarse. And then he wouldn't go no more. And Robina did not like it. Because Dick shouted swear words. He says they come naturally to you when you shout. And Robina said it was horrible. And that people would hear him. So we got out. And pushed him home. But he is very strong. And we were all very tired. And Robina says she hates him. Dick is going to give Mr. 'Opkins half a crown. To tell him how he makes him go. Because Mr. 'Opkins makes him gallop. Robina says it must be hypnotism. But Dick thinks it might be something simpler. I think Mr. 'Opkins very nice. He says you promised to lend him a book. What would help him to talk like a real country boy. So I have lent him a book about a window. By Mr. Bane. What came to see us last year. It has a lot of funny words in it. And he is going to learn them up. But he don't know what they mean. No more do I. I have written a lot of the book. It promises to be very interesting. It is all a dream. He is just the ordinary grown-up father. Neither better nor worse. And he goes up and up. It is a pleasant sensation. Till he reaches the moon. And there everything is different. It is the children that know everything. And are always right. And the grown-ups have to do all what they tell them. They are kind but firm. It is very good for him. And when he wakes up he is a better man. I put down everything that occurs to me. Like you suggested. There is quite a lot of it. And it makes you see how unjustly children are treated. They said I was to feed the donkey. Because it was my donkey. And I fed him. And there wasn't enough supper for Dick. And Dick said I was an idiot. And Robina said I wasn't to feed him. And in the morning there wasn't anything to feed him on. Because he won't eat anything but bread-and-butter. And the baker hadn't come. And he wasn't there. Because the man that comes to milk the cow had left the door open. And I was distracted. And Dick asked had I fed him. And of course I hadn't fed him. And lord how Dick talked. Never waited to hear anything, mind you. I let him talk. But it just shows you. We are all very happy. But shall be pleased to see you. Once again. The peppermint creams down here are not good. And are very dear. Compared with London prices. Isn't this a good letter? You said I was to always write just as I thought. So I'm doing it. I think that's all."

I read selections from this letter aloud to Ethelbertha. She said she was glad she had decided to come down with me.

IX

Had all things gone as ordered, our arrival at the St. Leonards' on Friday afternoon would have been imposing. It was our entrance, so to speak, upon the local stage; and Robina had decided it was a case where small economies ought not to be considered. The livery stable proprietor had suggested a brougham, but that would have necessitated one of us riding outside. I explained to Robina that, in the country, this was usual; and Robina had replied that much depended upon first impressions. Dick would, in all probability, claim the place for himself; and, the moment we were started, stick a pipe in his mouth. She selected an open landau of quite an extraordinary size, painted yellow. It looked to me an object more appropriate to a Lord Mayor's show than to the requirements of a Christian family; but Robina seemed touchy on the subject, and I said no more. It certainly was roomy. Old Glossop had turned it out well, with a pair of greys— seventeen hands, I judged them. The only thing that seemed wrong was the coachman. I can't explain why, but he struck me as the class of youth one associates with a milk-cart.

We set out at a gentle trot. Veronica, who had been in trouble most of the morning, sat stiffly on the extreme edge of her seat, clothed in the attitude of one dead to the world; Dick, in lavender gloves that Robina had thoughtfully bought for him, next to her. Ethelbertha, Robina, and myself sat perched on the back seat; to have leaned back would have been to lie down. Ethelbertha, having made up her mind she was going to dislike the whole family of the St. Leonards, seemed disinclined for conversation. Myself I had forgotten my cigar-case. I have tried the St. Leonard cigar. He does not smoke himself; but keeps a box for his friends. He tells me he fancies men are smoking cigars less than formerly. I did not see how I was going to get a smoke for the next three hours. Nothing annoys me more than being bustled and made to forget things. Robina, who has recently changed her views on the subject of freckles, shared a parasol with her mother. They had to hold it almost horizontally in front of them, and this obscured their view. I could not myself understand why people smiled as we went by. Apart from the carriage, which they must have seen before, we were not, I should have said, an exhilarating spectacle. A party of cyclists laughed outright. Robina said there was one thing we should have to be careful about, living in the country, and that was that the strong air and the loneliness combined didn't sap our intellect. She said she had noticed it—the tendency of country people to become prematurely silly. I did not share her fears, as I had by this time divined what it was that was amusing folks. Dick had discovered behind the cushions—remnant of some recent wedding, one supposes—a large and tastefully bound Book of Common Prayer. He and Veronica sat holding it between them. Looking at their faces one could almost hear the organ pealing.

Dick kept one eye on the parasol; and when, on passing into shade, it was lowered, he and Veronica were watching with rapt ecstasy the flight of swallows. Robina said she should tell Mr. Glossop of the insults to which respectable people were subject when riding in his carriage. She thought he ought to take steps to prevent it. She likewise suggested that the four of us, leaving the Little Mother in the carriage, should walk up the hill. Ethelbertha said that she herself would like a walk. She had been balancing herself on the edge of a cushion with her feet dangling for two miles, and was tired. She herself would have preferred a carriage made for ordinary-sized people. Our coachman called attention to the heat of the afternoon and the length of the hill, and recommended our remaining where we were; but his advice was dismissed as exhibiting want of feeling. Robina is, perhaps, a trifle over-sympathetic where animals are concerned. I remember, when they were children, her banging Dick over the head with the nursery bellows because he would not agree to talk in a whisper for fear of waking the cat. You can, of course, overdo kindness to animals, but it is a fault on the right side; and, as a rule, I do not discourage her. Veronica was allowed to remain, owing to her bad knee. It is a most unfortunate affliction. It comes on quite suddenly. There is nothing to be seen; but the child's face while she is suffering from it would move a heart of stone. It had been troubling her, so it appeared, all the morning; but she had said nothing, not wishing to alarm her mother. Ethelbertha, who thinks it may be hereditary—she herself having had an aunt who had suffered from contracted ligament—fixed her up as comfortably as the pain would permit with cushions in the centre of the back seat; and the rest of us toiled after the carriage.

I should not like to say for certain that horses have a sense of humour, but I sometimes think they must. I had a horse years ago who used to take delight in teasing girls. I can describe it no other way. He would pick out a girl a quarter of a mile off; always some haughty, well-dressed girl who was feeling pleased with herself. As we approached he would eye her with horror and astonishment. It was too marked to escape notice. A hundred yards off he would be walking sideways, backing away from her; I would see the poor lady growing scarlet with the insult and annoyance of it. Opposite to her, he would shy the entire width of the road, and make pretence to bolt. Looking back I would see her vainly appealing to surrounding nature for a looking-glass to see what it was that had gone wrong with her.

"What is the matter with me," she would be crying to herself; "that the very beasts of the field should shun me? Do they take me for a gollywog?"

Halfway up the hill, the off-side grey turned his head and looked at us. We were about a couple of hundred yards behind; it was a hot and dusty day. He whispered to the near-side grey, and the near-side grey turned and looked at us also. I knew what was coming. I've been played the same trick before. I shouted to the boy, but it was too late. They took the rest of the hill at a gallop and disappeared over the brow. Had there been an experienced coachman behind them, I should not have worried. Dick told his mother not to be alarmed, and started off at fifteen miles an hour. I calculated I was doing about ten, which for a gentleman past his first youth, in a frock suit designed to disguise rather than give play to the figure, I consider creditable. Robina, undecided whether to go on ahead with Dick or remain to assist her mother, wasted vigour by running from one to the other. Ethelbertha's one hope was that she might reach the wreckage in time to receive Veronica's last wishes.

It was in this order that we arrived at the St. Leonards'. Veronica, under an awning, sipping iced sherbet, appeared to be the centre of the party. She was recounting her experiences with a modesty that had already won all hearts. The rest of us, she had explained, had preferred walking, and would arrive later. She was evidently pleased to see me, and volunteered the information that the greys, to all seeming, had enjoyed their gallop.

I sent Dick back to break the good news to his mother. Young Bute said he would go too. He said he was fresher than Dick, and would get there first. As a matter of history he did, and was immediately sorry that he had.

This is not a well-ordered world, or it would not be our good deeds that would so often get us into trouble. Robina's insistence on our walking up the hill had been prompted by tender feeling for dumb animals: a virtuous emotion that surely the angels should have blessed. The result had been to bring down upon her suffering and reproach. It is not often that Ethelbertha loses her temper. When she does she makes use of the occasion to perform what one might describe as a mental spring-cleaning. All loose odds and ends of temper that may be lying about in her mind—any scrap of indignation that has been reposing peacefully, half forgotten, in a corner of her brain, she ferrets out and brushes into the general heap. Small annoyances of the year before last—little things she hadn't noticed at the time—incidents in your past life that, so far as you are concerned, present themselves as dim visions connected maybe with some previous existence, she whisks triumphantly into her pan. The method has its advantages. It leaves her, swept and garnished, without a scrap of ill-feeling towards any living soul. For quite a long period after one of these explosions it is impossible to get a cross word out of her. One has to wait sometimes for months. But while the clearing up is in progress the atmosphere round about is disturbing. The element of the whole thing is its comprehensive swiftness. Before they had reached the summit of the hill, Robina had acquired a tolerably complete idea of all she had done wrong since Christmas twelvemonth: the present afternoon's proceedings—including as they did the almost certain sacrificing of a sister to a violent death, together with the probable destruction of a father, no longer of an age to trifle with apoplexy—being but a fit and proper complement to what had gone before. It would be long, as Robina herself that evening bitterly declared, before she would again give ear to the promptings of her better nature.

To take next the sad case of Archibald Bute: his sole desire had been to relieve, at the earliest moment possible, the anxieties of a sister and a mother. Robina's new hat, not intended for sport, had broken away from its fastenings. With it, it had brought down her hair. There is a harmless contrivance for building up the female hair called, I am told, a pad. It can be made of combings, and then, of course, is literally the girl's own hair. He came upon Robina at the moment when, retracing her steps and with her back towards him, she was looking for it. With his usual luck, he was the first to find it. Ethelbertha thanked him for his information concerning Veronica, but seemed chiefly anxious to push on and convince herself that it was true. She took Dick's arm, and left Robina to follow on with Bute.

As I explained to him afterwards, had he stopped to ask my advice I should have counselled his leaving the job to Dick, who, after all, was only thirty seconds behind him. As regarded himself, I should have suggested his taking a walk in the opposite direction, returning, say, in half an hour, and pretending to have just arrived. By that time Robina, with the assistance of Janie's brush and comb, and possibly her powder-puff, would have been feeling herself again. He could have listened sympathetically to an account of the affair from Robina herself—her version, in which she would have appeared to advantage. Give her time, and she has a sense of humour. She would have made it bright and whimsical. Without asserting it in so many words, she would have conveyed the impression—I know her way— that she alone, throughout the whole commotion, had remained calm and helpful. "Dear old Dick" and "Poor dear papa"—I can hear her saying it—would have supplied the low comedy, and Veronica, alluded to with affection free from sentimentality, would have furnished the dramatic interest. It is not that Robina intends to mislead, but she has the artistic instinct. It would have made quite a charming story; Robina always the central figure. She would have enjoyed telling it, and would have been pleased with the person listening. All this—which would have been the reward of subterfuge—he had missed. Virtuous intention had gained for him nothing but a few scattered observations from Robina concerning himself; the probable object of his Creator in fashioning him—his relation to the scheme of things in general: observations all of which he had felt to be unjust.

We compared experiences over a pipe that same evening; and he told me of a friend of his, a law student, who had shared diggings with him in Edinburgh. A kinder-hearted young man, Bute felt sure, could never have breathed; nor one with a tenderer, more chivalrous regard for women; and the misery this brought him, to say nothing of the irritation caused to quite a number of respectable people, could hardly be imagined, so young Bute assured me, by anyone not personally acquainted with the parties. It was the plain and snappy girl, and the less attractive type of old maid, for whom he felt the most sorrow. He could not help thinking of all they had missed, and were likely to go on missing; the rapture—surely the woman's birthright—of feeling herself adored, anyhow, once in her life; the delight of seeing the lover's eye light up at her coming. Had he been a Mormon he would have married them all. They too—the neglected that none had invited to the feast of love—they also should know the joys of home, feel the sweet comfort of a husband's arm. Being a Christian, his power for good was limited. But at least he could lift from them the despairing conviction that they were outside the pale of masculine affection. Not one of them, so far as he could help it, but should be able to say:

"I—even I had a lover once. No, dear, we never married. It was one of those spiritual loves; a formal engagement with a ring would have spoiled it—coarsened it. No; it was just a beautiful thing that came into my life and passed away again, leaving behind it a fragrance that has sweetened all my days."

That is how he imagined they would talk about it, years afterwards, to the little niece or nephew, asking artless questions—how they would feel about it themselves. Whether law circles are peculiarly rich in unattractive spinsters, or whether it merely happened to be an exceptional season for them, Bute could not say; but certain it was that the number of sour-faced girls and fretful old maids in excess of the demand seemed to be greater than usual that winter in Edinburgh, with the result that young Hapgood had a busy time of it. He made love to them, not obtrusively, which might have laid them open to ridicule— many of them were old enough to have been his mother—but more by insinuation, by subtle suggestion. His feelings, so they gathered, were too deep for words; but the adoring eyes with which he would follow their every movement, the rapt ecstasy with which he would drink in their lightest remark about the weather, the tone of almost reverential awe with which he would enquire of them concerning their lesser ailments— all conveyed to their sympathetic observation the message that he dared not tell. He had no favourites. Sufficient it was that a woman should be unpleasant, for him to pour out at her feet the simulated passion of a lifetime. He sent them presents—nothing expensive—wrapped in pleasing pretence of anonymity; valentines carefully selected for their compromising character. One carroty-headed old maid with warts he had kissed upon the brow.

All this he did out of his great pity for them. It was a beautiful idea, but it worked badly. They did not understand—never got the hang of the thing: not one of them. They thought he was really gone on them. For a time his elusiveness, his backwardness in coming to the point, they attributed to a fit and proper fear of his fate; but as the months went by the feeling of each one was that he was carrying the apprehension of his own unworthiness too far. They gave him encouragement, provided for him "openings," till the wonder grew upon them how any woman ever did get married. At the end of their resources, they consulted bosom friends. In several instances the bosom friend turned out to be the bosom friend of more than one of them. The bosom friends began to take a hand in it. Some of them came to him with quite a little list, insisting—playfully at first—on his making up his mind what he was going to take and what he was going to leave; offering, as reward for prompt decision, to make things as easy for him as possible with the remainder of the column.

It was then he saw that his good intentions were likely to end in catastrophe. He would not tell the truth: that the whole scheme had been conceived out of charity towards all ill-constructed or dilapidated ladies; that personally he didn't care a hang for any of them; had only taken them on, vulgarly speaking, to give them a treat, and because nobody else would. That wasn't going to be a golden memory, colouring their otherwise drab existence. He explained that it was not love—not the love that alone would justify a man's asking of a woman that she should give herself to him for life—that he felt and always should feel for them, but merely admiration and deep esteem; and seventeen of them thought that would be sufficient to start with, and offered to chance the rest.

The truth had to come out. Friends who knew his noble nature could not sit by and hear him denounced as a heartless and eccentric profligate. Ladies whose beauty and popularity were beyond dispute thought it a touching and tender thing for him to have done; but every woman to whom he had ever addressed a kind word wanted to wring his neck.

He did the most sensible thing he could, under all the circumstances; changed his address to Aberdeen, where he had an aunt living. But the story followed him. No woman would be seen speaking to him. One admiring glance from Hapgood would send the prettiest girls home weeping to their mothers. Later on he fell in love—hopelessly, madly in love. But he dared not tell her—dared not let a living soul guess it. That was the only way he could show it. It is not sufficient, in this world, to want to do good; there's got to be a knack about it.

There was a man I met in Colorado, one Christmas-time. I was on a lecturing tour. His idea was to send a loving greeting to his wife in New York. He had been married nineteen years, and this was the first time he had been separated from his family on Christmas Day. He pictured them round the table in the little far-away New England parlour; his wife, his sister-in-law, Uncle Silas, Cousin Jane, Jack and Willy, and golden-haired Lena. They would be just sitting down to dinner, talking about him, most likely; wishing he were among them. They were a nice family and all fond of him. What joy it would give them to know that he was safe and sound; to hear the very tones of his loved voice speaking to them! Modern science has made possible these miracles. True, the long-distance telephone would cost him five dollars; but what is five dollars weighed against the privilege of wafting happiness to an entire family on Christmas Day! We had just come back from a walk. He slammed the money down, and laughed aloud at the thought of the surprise he was about to give them all.

The telephone bell rang out clear and distinct at the precise moment when his wife, with knife and fork in hand, was preparing to carve the turkey. She was a nervous lady, and twice that week had dreamed that she had seen her husband without being able to get to him. On the first occasion she had seen him enter a dry-goods store in Broadway, and hastening across the road had followed him in. He was hardly a dozen yards in front of her, but before she could overtake him all the young lady assistants had rushed from behind their counters and, forming a circle round her, had refused to let her pass, which in her dream had irritated her considerably. On the next occasion he had boarded a Brooklyn car in which she was returning home. She had tried to attract his attention with her umbrella, but he did not seem to see her; and every time she rose to go across to him the car gave a jerk and bumped her back into her seat. When she did get over to him it was not her husband at all, but the gentleman out of the Quaker Oats advertisement. She went to the telephone, feeling—as she said herself afterwards—all of a tremble.

That you could speak from Colorado to New York she would not then have believed had you told her. The thing was in its early stages, which may also have accounted for the voice reaching her strange and broken. I was standing beside him while he spoke. We were in the vestibule of the Savoy Hotel at Colorado Springs. It was five o'clock in the afternoon, which would be about seven in New York. He told her he was safe and well, and that she was not to fret about him. He told her he had been that morning for a walk in the Garden of the Gods, which is the name given to the local park; they do that sort of thing in Colorado. Also that he had drunk from the silicial springs abounding in that favoured land. I am not sure that "silicial" was the correct word. He was not sure himself: added to which he pronounced it badly. Whatever they were, he assured her they had done him good. He sent a special message to his Cousin Jane—a maiden lady of means—to the effect that she could rely upon seeing him soon. She was a touchy old lady, and liked to be singled out for special attention. He made the usual kind enquiries about everybody, sent them all his blessing, and only wished they could be with him in this delectable land where it seemed to be always sunshine and balmy breezes. He could have said more, but his time being up the telephone people switched him off; and feeling he had done a good and thoughtful deed, he suggested a game of billiards.

Could he have been a witness of events at the other end of the wire, his condition would have been one of less self-complacence. Long before the end of the first sentence his wife had come to the conclusion that this was a message from the dead. Why through a telephone did not greatly worry her. It seemed as reasonable a medium as any other she had ever heard of—indeed a trifle more so. Later, when she was able to review the matter calmly, it afforded her some consolation to reflect that things might have been worse. That "garden," together with the "silicial springs"—which she took to be "celestial," there was not much difference the way he pronounced it—was distinctly reassuring. The "eternal sunshine" and the "balmy breezes" likewise agreed with her knowledge of heavenly topography as derived from the Congregational Hymn-Book. That he should have needed to enquire concerning the health of herself and the children had puzzled her. The only explanation was that they didn't know everything, not even up. There—may be, not the new-comers. She had answered as coherently as her state of distraction would permit, and had then dropped limply to the floor. It was the sound of her falling against the umbrella-stand and upsetting it that brought them all trooping out from the dining-room.

It took her some time to get the thing home to them; and when she had finished, her brother Silas, acting on the impulse of the moment, rang up the Exchange, with some vague idea of getting into communication with St. Peter and obtaining further particulars, but recollected himself in time to explain to the "hulloa girl" that he had made a mistake.

The eldest boy, a practical youth, pointed out, very sensibly, that nothing could be gained by their not going on with their dinner, but was bitterly reproached for being able to think of any form of enjoyment at a moment when his poor dear father was in heaven.

It reminded his mother of the special message to Cousin Jane, who up to that moment had been playing the part of comforter. With the collapse of Cousin Jane, dramatic in its suddenness, conversation disappeared. At nine o'clock the entire family went dinnerless to bed.

The eldest boy—as I have said, a practical youth—had the sense to get up early the next morning and send a wire, which brought the glad news back to them that their beloved one was not in heaven, but was still in Colorado. But the only reward my friend got for all his tender thoughtfulness was the vehement injunction never for the remainder of his life to play such a fool's trick again.

There were other cases I could have recited showing the ill recompense that so often overtakes the virtuous action; but, as I explained to Bute, it would have saddened me to dwell upon the theme.

It was quite a large party assembled at the St. Leonards', including one or two county people, and I should have liked, myself, to have made a better entrance. A large lady with a very small voice seemed to be under the impression that I had arranged the whole business on purpose. She said it was "so dramatic." One good thing came out of it: Janie, in her quiet, quick way, saw to it that Ethelbertha and Robina slipped into the house unnoticed by way of the dairy. When they joined the other guests, half an hour later, they had had a cup of tea and a rest, and were feeling calm and cool, with their hair nicely done; and Ethelbertha remarked to Robina on the way home what a comfort it must be to Mrs. St. Leonard to have a daughter so capable, one who knew just the right thing to do, and did it without making a fuss and a disturbance.

Everyone was very nice. Of course we made the usual mistake: they talked to me about books and plays, and I gave them my views on agriculture and cub-hunting. I'm not quite sure what fool it was who described a bore as a man who talked about himself. As a matter of fact it is the only subject the average man knows sufficiently well to make interesting. There's a man I know; he makes a fortune out of a patent food for infants. He began life as a dairy farmer, and hit upon it quite by accident. When he talks about the humours of company promoting and the tricks of the advertising agent he is amusing. I have sat at his table, when he was a bachelor, and listened to him by the hour with enjoyment. The mistake he made was marrying a broad-minded, cultured woman, who ruined him—conversationally, I mean. He is now well-informed and tiresome on most topics. That is why actors and actresses are always such delightful company: they are not ashamed to talk about themselves. I remember a dinner-party once: our host was one of the best-known barristers in London. A famous lady novelist sat on his right, and a scientist of world-wide reputation had the place of honour next our hostess, who herself had written a history of the struggle for nationality in South America that serves as an authority to all the Foreign Offices in Europe. Among the remaining guests were a bishop, the editor-in-chief of a London daily newspaper, a man who knew the interior of China as well as most men know their own club, a Russian revolutionist just escaped from Siberia, a leading dramatist, a Cabinet Minister, and a poet whose name is a household word wherever the English tongue is spoken. And for two hours we sat and listened to a wicked-looking little woman who from the boards of a Bowery music-hall had worked her way up to the position of a star in musical comedy. Education, as she observed herself without regret, had not been compulsory throughout the waterside district of Chicago in her young days; and, compelled to earn her own living from the age of thirteen, opportunity for supplying the original deficiency had been wanting. But she knew her subject, which was Herself—her experiences, her reminiscences: and bad sense enough to stick to it. Until the moment when she took "the liberty of chipping in," to use her own expression, the amount of twaddle talked had been appalling. The bishop had told us all he had learnt about China during a visit to San Francisco, while the man who had spent the last twenty years of his life in the country was busy explaining his views on the subject of the English drama. Our hostess had been endeavouring to make the scientist feel at home by talking to him about radium. The dramatist had explained at some length his views of the crisis in Russia. The poet had quite spoilt his dinner trying to suggest to the Cabinet Minister new sources of taxation. The Russian revolutionist had told us what ought to have been a funny story about a duck; and the lady novelist and the Cabinet Minister had discussed Christian Science for a quarter of an hour, each under the mistaken impression that the other one was a believer in it. The editor had been explaining the attitude of the Church towards the New Theology; and our host, one of the wittiest men at the Bar, had been talking chiefly to the butler. The relief of listening to anybody talking about something they knew was like finding a match-box to a man who has been barking his shins in the dark. For the rest of the dinner we clung to her.

I could have made myself quite interesting to these good squires and farmers talking to them about theatres and the literary celebrities I have met; and they could have told me dog stories and given me useful information as to the working of the Small Holdings Act. They said some very charming things about my books—mostly to the effect that they read and enjoyed them when feeling ill or suffering from mental collapse. I gathered that had they always continued in a healthy state of mind and body it would not have occurred to them to read me. One man assured me I had saved his life. It was his brain, he told me. He had been so upset by something that had happened to him that he had almost lost his reason. There were times when he could not even remember his own name; his mind seemed an absolute blank. And then one day by chance—or Providence, or whatever you choose to call it—he had taken up a book of mine. It was the only thing he had been able to read for months and months! And now, whenever he felt himself run down—his brain like a squeezed orange (that was his simile)—he would put everything else aside and read a book of mine—any one: it didn't matter which. I suppose one ought to be glad that one has saved somebody's life; but I should like to have the choosing of them myself.

I am not sure that Ethelbertha is going to like Mrs. St. Leonard; and I don't think Mrs. St. Leonard will much like Ethelbertha. I have gathered that Mrs. St. Leonard doesn't like anybody much—except, of course, when it is her duty. She does not seem to have the time. Man is born to trouble, and it is not bad philosophy to get oneself accustomed to the feeling. But Mrs. St. Leonard has given herself up to the pursuit of trouble to the exclusion of all other interests in life. She appears to regard it as the only calling worthy a Christian woman. I found her alone one afternoon. Her manner was preoccupied; I asked if I could be of any assistance.

"No," she answered, "I am merely trying to think what it can be that has been worrying me all the morning. It has clean gone out of my head."

She remembered it a little later with a glad sigh.

St. Leonard himself, Ethelbertha thinks charming. We are to go again on Sunday for her to see the children. Three or four people we met I fancy we shall be able to fit in with. We left at half-past six, and took Bute back with us to supper.

X

S he's a good woman," said Robina.

"Who's a good woman?" I asked.

"He's trying, I expect; although he is an old dear: to live with, I mean," continued Robina, addressing apparently the rising moon. "And then there are all those children."

"You are thinking of Mrs. St. Leonard," I suggested.

"There seems no way of making her happy," explained Robina. "On Thursday I went round early in the morning to help Janie pack the baskets for the picnic. It was her own idea, the picnic."

"Speaking of picnics," I said.

"You might have thought," went on Robina, "that she was dressing for her own funeral. She said she knew she was going to catch her death of cold, sitting on the wet grass. Something told her. I reminded her it hadn't rained for three weeks, and that everything was as dry as a bone, but she said that made no difference to grass. There is always a moisture in grass, and that cushions and all that only helped to draw it out. Not that it mattered. The end had to come, and so long as the others were happy—you know her style. Nobody ever thought of her. She was to be dragged here, dragged there. She talked about herself as if she were some sacred image. It got upon my nerves at last, so that I persuaded Janie to let me offer to stop at home with her. I wasn't too keen about going myself; not by that time."

"When our desires leave us, says Rochefoucauld," I remarked, "we pride ourselves upon our virtue in having overcome them."

"Well, it was her fault, anyhow," retorted Robina; "and I didn't make a virtue of it. I told her I'd just as soon not go, and that I felt sure the others would be all right without her, so that there was no need for her to be dragged anywhere. And then she burst into tears."

"She said," I suggested, "that it was hard on her to have children who could wish to go to a picnic and leave their mother at home; that it was little enough enjoyment she had in her life, heaven knows; that if there was one thing she had been looking forward to it was this day's outing; but still, of course, if everybody would be happier without her—"

"Something of the sort," admitted Robina; "only there was a lot of it. We had to all fuss round her, and swear that without her it wouldn't be worth calling a picnic. She brightened up on the way home."

The screech-owl in the yew-tree emitted a blood-curdling scream. He perches there each evening on the extreme end of the longest bough. Dimly outlined against the night, he has the appearance of a friendly hobgoblin. But I wish he didn't fancy himself as a vocalist. It is against his own interests, I am sure, if he only knew it. That American college yell of his must have the effect of sending every living thing within half a mile back into its hole. Maybe it is a provision of nature for clearing off the very old mice who have become stone deaf and would otherwise be a burden on their relatives. The others, unless out for suicide, must, one thinks, be tolerably safe. Ethelbertha is persuaded he is a sign of death; but seeing there isn't a square quarter of a mile in this county without its screech-owl, there can hardly by this time be a resident that an Assurance Society would look at. Veronica likes him. She even likes his screech. I found her under the tree the other night, wrapped up in a shawl, trying to learn it. As if one of them were not enough! It made me quite cross with her. Besides, it wasn't a bit like it, as I told her. She said it was better than I could do, anyhow; and I was idiot enough to take up the challenge. It makes me angry now, when I think of it: a respectable, middle-aged literary man, standing under a yew-tree trying to screech like an owl. And the bird was silly enough to encourage us.

"She was a charming girl," I said, "seven-and-twenty years ago, when St. Leonard fell in love with her. She had those dark, dreamy eyes so suggestive of veiled mysteries; and her lips must have looked bewitching when they pouted. I expect they often did. They do so still; but the pout of a woman of forty-six no longer fascinates. To a pretty girl of nineteen a spice of temper, an illogical unreasonableness, are added attractions: the scratch of a blue-eyed kitten only tempts us to tease her the more. Young Hubert St. Leonard—he had curly brown hair, with a pretty trick of blushing, and was going to conquer the world—found her fretfulness, her very selfishness adorable: and told her so, kneeling before her, gazing into her bewildering eyes—only he called it her waywardness, her imperiousness; begged her for his sake to be more capricious. Told her how beautiful she looked when displeased. So, no doubt, she did—at nineteen."

"He didn't tell you all that, did he?" demanded Robina.

"Not a word," I reassured her, "except that she was acknowledged by all authorities to have been the most beautiful girl in Tunbridge Wells, and that her father had been ruined by a rascally solicitor. No, I was merely, to use the phrase of the French police courts, 'reconstructing the crime.'"

"It may be all wrong," grumbled Robina.

"It may be," I agreed. "But why? Does it strike you as improbable?"

We were sitting in the porch, waiting for Dick to come by the white path across the field.

"No," answered Robina. "It all sounds very probable. I wish it didn't."

"You must remember," I continued, "that I am an old playgoer. I have sat out so many of this world's dramas. It is as easy to reconstruct them backwards as forwards. We are witnessing the last act of the St. Leonard drama: that unsatisfactory last act that merely fills out time after the play is ended! The intermediate acts were probably more exciting, containing 'passionate scenes' played with much earnestness; chiefly for the amusement of the servants. But the first act, with the Kentish lanes and woods for a back-cloth, must have been charming. Here was the devout lover she had heard of, dreamed of. It is delightful to be regarded as perfection—not absolute perfection, for that might put a strain upon us to live up to, but as so near perfection that to be more perfect would just spoil it. The spots upon us, that unappreciative friends and relations would magnify into blemishes, seen in their true light: artistic shading relieving a faultlessness that might otherwise prove too glaring. Dear Hubert found her excellent just as she was in every detail. It would have been a crime against Love for her to seek to change herself."

"Well, then, it was his fault," argued Robina. "If he was silly enough to like her faults, and encourage her in them—"

"What could he have done," I asked, "even if he had seen them? A lover does not point out his mistress's shortcomings to her."

"Much the more sensible plan if he did," insisted Robina. "Then if she cared for him she could set to work to cure herself."

"You would like it?" I said; "you would appreciate it in your own case? Can you imagine young Bute—?"

"Why young Bute?" demanded Robina; "what's he got to do with it?"

"Nothing," I answered; "except that he happens to be the first male creature you have ever come across since you were six that you haven't flirted with."

"I don't flirt with them," said Robina; "I merely try to be nice to them."

"With the exception of young Bute," I persisted.

"He irritates me," Robina explained.

"I was reading," I said, "the other day, an account of the marriage customs prevailing among the Lower Caucasians. The lover takes his stand beneath his lady's window, and, having attracted her attention, proceeds to sing. And if she seems to like it—if she listens to it without getting mad, that means she doesn't want him. But if she gets upset about it—slams down the window and walks away, then it's all right. I think it's the Lower Caucasians."

"Must be a very silly people," said Robina; "I suppose a pail of water would be the highest proof of her affection he could hope for."

"A complex being, man," I agreed. "We will call him X. Can you imagine young X coming to you and saying: 'My dear Robina, you have many excellent qualities. You can be amiable—so long as you are having your own way in everything; but thwarted you can be just horrid. You are very kind—to those who are willing for you to be kind to them in your own way, which is not always their way. You can be quite unselfish—when you happen to be in an unselfish mood, which is far from frequent. You are capable and clever, but, like most capable and clever people, impatient and domineering; highly energetic when not feeling lazy; ready to forgive the moment your temper is exhausted. You are generous and frank, but if your object could only be gained through meanness or deceit you would not hesitate a moment longer than was necessary to convince yourself that the circumstances justified the means. You are sympathetic, tender-hearted, and have a fine sense of justice; but I can see that tongue of yours, if not carefully watched, wearing decidedly shrewish. You have any amount of grit. A man might go tiger-hunting with you—with no one better; but you are obstinate, conceited, and exacting. In short, to sum you up, you have all the makings in you of an ideal wife combined with faults sufficient to make a Socrates regret he'd ever married you.'"

"Yes, I would!" said Robina, springing to her feet. I could not see her face, but I knew there was the look upon it that made Primgate want to paint her as Joan of Arc; only it would never stop long enough. "I'd love him for talking like that. And I'd respect him. If he was that sort of man I'd pray God to help me to be the sort of woman he wanted me to be. I'd try. I'd try all day long. I would!"

"I wonder," I said. Robina had surprised me. I admit it. I thought I knew the sex better.

"Any girl would," said Robina. "He'd be worth it."

"It would be a new idea," I mused. "*Gott im Himmel*! what a new world might it not create!" The fancy began to take hold of me. "Love no longer blind. Love refusing any more to be the poor blind fool—sport of gods and men. Love no longer passion's slave. His bonds broken, the senseless bandage flung aside. Love helping life instead of muddling it. Marriage, the foundation of civilisation, no longer reared upon the sands of lies and illusions, but grappled to the rock of truth—reality. Have you ever read 'Tom Jones?'" I said.

"No," answered Robina; "I've always heard it wasn't a nice book."

"It isn't," I said. "Man isn't a nice animal, not all of him. Nor woman either. There's a deal of the beast in man. What can you expect? Till a few paltry thousands of years ago he *was* a beast, fighting with other beasts, his fellow denizens of the woods and caves; watching for his prey, crouched in the long grass of the river's bank, tearing it with claws and teeth, growling as he ate. So he lived and died through the dim unnamed ages, transmitting his beast's blood, his bestial instincts, to his offspring, growing ever stronger, fiercer, from generation to generation, while the rocks piled up their strata and the oceans shaped their beds. Moses! Why, Lord Rothschild's great-grandfather, a few score times removed, must have known Moses, talked with him. Babylon! It is a modern city, fallen into disuse for the moment, owing to alteration of traffic routes. History! it is a tale of to-day. Man was crawling about the world on all fours, learning to be an animal for millions of years before the secret of his birth was whispered to him. It is only during the last few centuries that he has been trying to be a man. Our modern morality! Why, compared with the teachings of nature, it is but a few days old. What do you expect? That he shall forget the lessons of the æons at the bidding of the hours?"

"Then you advise me to read 'Tom Jones'?" said Robina.

"Yes," I said, "I do. I should not if I thought you were still a child, knowing only blind trust, or blind terror. The sun is not extinguished because occasionally obscured by mist; the scent of the rose is not dead because of the worm in the leaf. A healthy rose can afford a few worms—has got to, anyhow. All men are not Tom Joneses. The standard of masculine behaviour continues to go up: many of us make fine efforts to conform to it, and some of us succeed. But the Tom Jones is there in all of us who are not anæmic or consumptive. And there's no sense at all in getting cross with us about it, because we cannot help it. We are doing our best. In another hundred thousand years or so, provided all goes well, we shall be the perfect man. And seeing our early training, I flatter myself that, up to the present, we have done remarkably well."

"Nothing like being satisfied with oneself," said Robina.

"I'm not satisfied," I said; "I'm only hopeful. But it irritates me when I hear people talk as though man had been born a white-souled angel and was making supernatural efforts to become a sinner. That seems to me the way to discourage him. What he wants is bucking up; somebody to say to him, 'Bravo! why, this is splendid! Just think, my boy, what you were, and that not so very long ago—an unwashed, hairy savage; your law that of the jungle, your morals those of the rabbit-warren. Now look at yourself—dressed in your little shiny hat, your trousers neatly creased, walking with your wife to church on Sunday! Keep on—that's all you've got to do. In a few more centuries your own mother Nature won't know you.'

"You women," I continued; "why, a handful of years ago we bought and sold you, kept you in cages, took the stick to you when you were not spry in doing what you were told. Did you ever read the history of Patient Griselda?"

"Yes," said Robina, "I have." I gathered from her tone that the Joan of Arc expression had departed. Had Primgate wanted to paint her at that particular moment I should have suggested Katherine—during the earlier stages—listening to a curtain lecture from Petruchio. "Are you suggesting that all women should take her for a model?"

"No," I said, "I'm not. Though were we living in Chaucer's time I might; and you would not think it even silly. What I'm impressing upon you is that the human race has yet a little way to travel before the average man can be regarded as an up-to-date edition of King Arthur—the King Arthur of the poetical legend, I mean. Don't be too impatient with him."

"Thinking what a beast he has been ought to make him impatient himself with himself," considered Robina. "He ought to be feeling so ashamed of himself as to be willing to do anything."

The owl in the old yew screamed, whether with indignation or amusement I cannot tell.

"And woman," I said, "had the power been hers, would she have used it to sweeter purpose? Where is your evidence? Your Cleopatras, Pompadours, Jezebels; your Catherines of Russia, late Empresses of China; your Faustines of all ages and all climes; your Mother Brownriggs; your Lucretia Borgias, Salomes—I could weary you with names. Your Roman task-mistresses; your drivers of lodging-house slaveys; your ladies who whipped their pages to death in the Middle Ages; your modern dames of fashion, decked with the plumage of the tortured grove. There have been other women also—noble women, their names like beacon-lights studding the dark waste of history. So there have been noble men—saints, martyrs, heroes. The sex-line divides us physically, not morally. Woman has been man's accomplice in too many crimes to claim to be his judge. 'Male and female created He them'—like and like, for good and evil."

By good fortune I found a loose match. I lighted a fresh cigar.

"Dick, I suppose, is the average man," said Robina.

"Most of us are," I said, "when we are at home. Carlyle was the average man in the little front parlour in Cheyne Row, though, to hear fools talk, you might think no married couple outside literary circles had ever been known to exchange a cross look. So was Oliver Cromwell in his own palace with the door shut. Mrs. Cromwell must have thought him monstrous silly, placing sticky sweetmeats for his guests to sit on—told him so, most likely. A cheery, kindly man, notwithstanding, though given to moods. He and Mrs. Cromwell seem to have rubbed along, on the whole, pretty well together. Old Sam Johnson—great, God-fearing, lovable, cantankerous old brute! Life with him, in a small house on a limited income, must have had its ups and downs. Milton and Frederick the Great were, one hopes, a little below the average. Did their best, no doubt; lacked understanding. Not so easy as it looks, living up to the standard of the average man. Very clever people, in particular, find it tiring."

"I shall never marry," said Robina. "At least, I hope I sha'n't."

"Why 'hope'?" I asked.

"Because I hope I shall never be idiot enough," she answered. "I see it all so clearly. I wish I didn't. Love! it's only an ugly thing with a pretty name. It will not be me that he will fall in love with. He will not know me until it is too late. How can he? It will be merely with the outside of me—my pink-and-white skin, my rounded arms. I feel it sometimes when I see men looking at me, and it makes me mad. And at other times the admiration in their eyes pleases me. And that makes me madder still."

The moon had slipped behind the wood. She had risen, and, leaning against the porch, was standing with her hands clasped. I fancy she had forgotten me. She seemed to be talking to the night.

"It's only a trick of Nature to make fools of us," she said. "He will tell me I am all the world to him; that his love will outlive the stars—will believe it himself at the time, poor fellow! He will call me a hundred pretty names, will kiss my feet and hands. And if I'm fool enough to listen to him, it may last"—she laughed; it was rather an ugly laugh— "six months; with luck perhaps a year, if I'm careful not to go out in the east wind and come home with a red nose, and never let him catch me in curl papers. It will not be me that he will want: only my youth, and the novelty of me, and the mystery. And when that is gone—"

She turned to me. It was a strange face I saw then in the pale light, quite a fierce little face. She laid her hands upon my shoulders, and I felt them cold. "What comes when it is dead?" she said. "What follows? You must know. Tell me. I want the truth."

Her vehemence had arisen so suddenly. The little girl I had set out to talk with was no longer there. To my bewilderment, it was a woman that was questioning me.

I drew her down beside me. But the childish face was still stern.

"I want the truth," she said; so that I answered very gravely:

"When the passion is passed; when the glory and the wonder of Desire—Nature's eternal ritual of marriage, solemnising, sanctifying it to her commands—is ended; when, sooner or later, some grey dawn finds you wandering bewildered in once familiar places, seeking vainly the lost palace of youth's dreams; when Love's frenzy is faded, like the fragrance of the blossom, like the splendour of the dawn; there will remain to you, just what was there before—no more, no less. If passion was all you had to give to one another, God help you. You have had your hour of madness. It is finished. If greed of praise and worship was your price—well, you have had your payment. The bargain is complete. If mere hope to be made happy was your lure, one pities you. We do not make each other happy. Happiness is the gift of the gods, not of man. The secret lies within you, not without. What remains to you will depend not upon what you *thought*, but upon what you *are*. If behind the lover there was the man—behind the impossible goddess of his love-sick brain some honest, human woman, then life lies not behind you, but before you.

"Life is giving, not getting. That is the mistake we most of us set out with. It is the work that is the joy, not the wages; the game, not the score. The lover's delight is to yield, not to claim. The crown of motherhood is pain. To serve the State at cost of ease and leisure; to spend his thought

JEROME K. JEROME

and labour upon a hundred schemes, is the man's ambition. Life is doing, not having. It is to gain the peak the climber strives, not to possess it. Fools marry thinking what they are going to get out of it: good store of joys and pleasure, opportunities for self-indulgence, eternal soft caresses—the wages of the wanton. The rewards of marriage are toil, duty, responsibility—manhood, womanhood. Love's baby talk you will have outgrown. You will no longer be his 'Goddess,' 'Angel,' 'Popsy Wopsy,' 'Queen of his heart.' There are finer names than these: wife, mother, priestess in the temple of humanity. Marriage is renunciation, the sacrifice of Self upon the altar of the race. 'A trick of Nature' you call it. Perhaps. But a trick of Nature compelling you to surrender yourself to the purposes of God."

I fancy we must have sat in silence for quite a long while; for the moon, creeping upward past the wood, had flooded the fields again with light before Robina spoke.

"Then all love is needless," she said, "we could do better without it, choose with more discretion. If it is only something that worries us for a little while and then passes, what is the sense of it?"

"You could ask the same question of Life itself," I said; "'something that worries us for a little while, then passes.' Perhaps the 'worry,' as you call it, has its uses. Volcanic upheavals are necessary to the making of a world. Without them the ground would remain rock-bound, unfitted for its purposes. That explosion of Youth's pent-up forces that we term Love serves to the making of man and woman. It does not die, it takes new shape. The blossom fades as the fruit forms. The passion passes to give place to peace. The trembling lover has become the helper, the comforter, the husband."

"But the failures," Robina persisted; "I do not mean the silly or the wicked people; but the people who begin by really loving one another, only to end in disliking—almost hating one another. How do *they* get there?"

"Sit down," I said, "and I will tell you a story.

"Once upon a time there was a girl, and a boy who loved her. She was a clever, brilliant girl, and she had the face of an angel. They lived near to one another, seeing each other almost daily. But the boy, awed by the difference of their social position, kept his secret, as he thought, to himself; dreaming, as youth will, of the day when fame and wealth would bridge the gulf between them. The kind look in her eyes, the occasional seeming pressure of her hand, he allowed to feed his hopes;

and on the morning of his departure for London an incident occurred that changed his vague imaginings to set resolve. He had sent on his scanty baggage by the carrier, intending to walk the three miles to the station. It was early in the morning, and he had not expected to meet a soul. But a mile from the village he overtook her. She was reading a book, but she made no pretence that the meeting was accidental, leaving him to form what conclusions he would. She walked with him some distance, and he told her of his plans and hopes; and she answered him quite simply that she should always remember him, always be more glad than she could tell to hear of his success. Near the end of the lane they parted, she wishing him in that low sweet woman's voice of hers all things good. He turned, a little farther on, and found that she had also turned. She waved her hand to him, smiling. And through the long day's journey and through many days to come there remained with him that picture of her, bringing with it the scent of the pine-woods: her white hand waving to him, her sweet eyes smiling wistfully.

"But fame and fortune are not won so quickly as boys dream, nor is life as easy to live bravely as it looks in visions. It was nearly twenty years before they met again. Neither had married. Her people were dead and she was living alone; and to him the world at last had opened her doors. She was still beautiful. A gracious, gentle lady, she had grown; clothed with that soft sweet dignity that Time bestows upon rare women, rendering them fairer with the years.

"To the man it seemed a miracle. The dream of those early days came back to him. Surely there was nothing now to separate them. Nothing had changed but the years, bringing to them both wider sympathies, calmer, more enduring emotions. She welcomed him again with the old kind smile, a warmer pressure of the hand; and, allowing a little time to pass for courtesy's sake, he told her what was the truth: that he had never ceased to love her, never ceased to keep the vision of her fair pure face before him, his ideal of all that man could find of help in womanhood. And her answer, until years later he read the explanation, remained a mystery to him. She told him that she loved him, that she had never loved any other man and never should; that his love, for so long as he chose to give it to her, she should always prize as the greatest gift of her life. But with that she prayed him to remain content.

"He thought perhaps it was a touch of woman's pride, of hurt dignity that he had kept silent so long, not trusting her; that perhaps as time went by she would change her mind. But she never did; and after awhile,

JEROME K. JEROME

finding that his persistence only pained her, he accepted the situation. She was not the type of woman about whom people talk scandal, nor would it have troubled her much had they done so. Able now to work where he would, he took a house in a neighbouring village, where for the best part of the year he lived, near to her. And to the end they remained lovers."

"I think I understand," said Robina. "I will tell you afterwards if I am wrong."

"I told the story to a woman many years ago," I said, "and she also thought she understood. But she was only half right."

"We will see," said Robina. "Go on."

"She left a letter, to be given to him after her death, in case he survived her; if not, to be burned unopened. In it she told him her reason, or rather her reasons, for having refused him. It was an odd letter. The 'reasons' sounded so pitiably insufficient. Until one took the pains to examine them in the cold light of experience. And then her letter struck one, not as foolish, but as one of the grimmest commentaries upon marriage that perhaps had ever been penned.

"It was because she had wished always to remain his ideal; to keep their love for one another to the end, untarnished; to be his true helpmeet in all things, that she had refused to marry him.

"Had he spoken that morning she had waited for him in the lane— she had half hoped, half feared it—she might have given her promise: 'For Youth,' so she wrote, 'always dreams it can find a new way.' She thanked God that he had not.

"'Sooner or later,' so ran the letter, 'you would have learned, Dear, that I was neither saint nor angel; but just a woman—such a tiresome, inconsistent creature; she would have exasperated you—full of a thousand follies and irritabilities that would have marred for you all that was good in her. I wanted you to have of me only what was worthy, and this seemed the only way. Counting the hours to your coming, hating the pain of your going, I could always give to you my best. The ugly words, the whims and frets that poison speech—they could wait; it was my lover's hour.

"'And you, Dear, were always so tender, so gay. You brought me joy with both your hands. Would it have been the same, had you been my husband? How could it? There were times, even as it was, when you vexed me. Forgive me, Dear, I mean it was my fault—ways of thought and action that did not fit in with my ways, that I was not large-minded enough to pass over. As my lover, they were but as spots upon the sun. It was easy to control the momentary irritation that they caused me. Time was too precious for even a moment of estrangement. As my husband, the jarring note would have been continuous, would have widened into discord. You see, Dear, I was not great enough to love *all* of you. I remember, as a child, how indignant I always felt with God when my nurse told me He would not love me because I was naughty, that He only loved good children. It seemed such a poor sort of love, that. Yet that is precisely how we men and women do love; taking only what gives us pleasure, repaying the rest with anger. There would have arisen the unkind words that can never be recalled; the ugly silences; the gradual withdrawing from one another. I dared not face it.

"'It was not all selfishness. Truthfully I can say I thought more of you than of myself. I wanted to keep the shadows of life away from you. We men and women are like the flowers. It is in sunshine that we come to our best. You were my hero. I wanted you to be great. I wanted you to be surrounded by lovely dreams. I wanted your love to be a thing holy, helpful to you.'

"It was a long letter. I have given you the gist of it."

Again there was a silence between us.

"You think she did right?" asked Robina.

"I cannot say," I answered; "there are no rules for Life, only for the individual."

"I have read it somewhere," said Robina—"where was it?—'Love suffers all things, and rejoices.'"

"Maybe in old Thomas Kempis. I am not sure," I said.

"It seems to me," said Robina, "that the explanation lies in that one sentence of hers: 'I was not great enough to love *all* of you.'"

"It seems to me," I said, "that the whole art of marriage is the art of getting on with the other fellow. It means patience, self-control, forbearance. It means the laying aside of our self-conceit and admitting to ourselves that, judged by eyes less partial than our own, there may be much in us that is objectionable, that calls for alteration. It means toleration for views and opinions diametrically opposed to our most cherished convictions. It means, of necessity, the abandonment of many habits and indulgences that however trivial have grown to be important to us. It means the shaping of our own desires to the needs of others; the acceptance often of surroundings and conditions personally distasteful to us. It means affection deep and strong enough to bear away the ugly things of life—its quarrels, wrongs, misunderstandings—swiftly and silently into the sea of forgetfulness. It means courage, good humour, commonsense."

"That is what I am saying," explained Robina. "It means loving him even when he's naughty."

Dick came across the fields. Robina rose and slipped into the house.

"You are looking mighty solemn, Dad," said Dick.

"Thinking of Life, Dick," I confessed. "Of the meaning and the explanation of it."

"Yes, it's a problem, Life," admitted Dick.

"A bit of a teaser," I agreed.

We smoked in silence for awhile.

"Loving a good woman must be a tremendous help to a man," said Dick.

He looked very handsome, very gallant, his boyish face flashing challenge to the Fates.

"Tremendous, Dick," I agreed.

Robina called to him that his supper was ready. He knocked the ashes from his pipe, and followed her into the house. Their laughing voices came to me broken through the half-closed doors. From the night around me rose a strange low murmur. It seemed to me as though above the silence I heard the far-off music of the Mills of God.

XI

I fancy Veronica is going to be an authoress. Her mother thinks this may account for many things about her that have been troubling us. The story never got far. It was laid aside for the more alluring work of play-writing, and apparently forgotten. I came across the copy-book containing her "Rough Notes" the other day. There is decided flavour about them. I transcribe selections; the spelling, as before, being my own.

"The scene is laid in the Moon. But everything is just the same as down here. With one exception. The children rule. The grown-ups do not like it. But they cannot help it. Something has happened to them. They don't know what. And the world is as it used to be. In the sweet old story-books. Before sin came. There are fairies that dance o' nights. And Witches. That lure you. And then turn you into things. And a dragon who lives in a cave. And springs out at people. And eats them. So that you have to be careful. And all the animals talk. And there are giants. And lots of magic. And it is the children who know everything. And what to do for it. And they have to teach the grown-ups. And the grown-ups don't believe half of it. And are far too fond of arguing. Which is a sore trial to the children. But they have patience, and are just.

"Of course the grown-ups have to go to school. They have much to learn. Poor things! And they hate it. They take no interest in fairy lore. And what would happen to them if they got wrecked on a Desert Island they don't seem to care. And then there are languages. What they will need when they come to be children. And have to talk to all the animals. And magic. Which is deep. And they hate it. And say it is rot. They are full of tricks. One catches them reading trashy novels. Under the desk. All about love. Which is wasting their children's money. And God knows it is hard enough to earn. But the children are not angry with them. Remembering how they felt themselves. When they were grown up. Only firm.

"The children give them plenty of holidays. Because holidays are good for everyone. They freshen you up. But the grown-ups are very stupid. And do not care for sensible games. Such as Indians. And Pirates. What would sharpen their faculties. And so fit them for the future. They only care to play with a ball. Which is of no help. To the stern realities of life. Or talk. Lord, how they talk!

"There is one grown-up. Who is very clever. He can talk about everything. But it leads to nothing. And spoils the party. So they send him to bed. And there are two grown-ups. A male and a female. And they talk love. All the time. Even on fine days. Which is maudlin. But the children are patient with them. Knowing it takes all sorts. To make a world. And trusting they will grow out of it. And of course there are grown-ups who are good. And a comfort to their children.

"And everything the children like is good. And wholesome. And everything the grown-ups like is bad for them. *And they mustn't have it*. They clamour for tea and coffee. What undermines their nervous system. And waste their money in the tuck shop. Upon chops. And turtle soup. And the children have to put them to bed. And give them pills. Till they feel better.

"There is a little girl named Prue. Who lives with a little boy named Simon. They mean well. But haven't much sense. They have two grown-ups. A male and a female. Named Peter and Martha. Respectively. They are just the ordinary grown-ups. Neither better nor worse. And much might be done with them. By kindness. But Prue and Simon *go the wrong way to work*. It is blame blame blame all day long. But as for praise. Oh never!

"One summer's day Prue and Simon take Peter for a walk. In the country. And they meet a cow. And they think this a good opportunity. To test Peter's knowledge. Of languages. So they tell him to talk to the cow. And he talks to the cow. And the cow don't understand him. And he don't understand the cow. And they are mad with him. 'What is the use,' they say. 'Of our paying expensive fees. To have you taught the language. By a first-class cow. And when you come out into the country. You can't talk it.' And he says he did talk it. But they will not listen to him. But go on raving. And in the end it turns out. *It was a Jersey cow*! What talked a dialect. So of course he couldn't understand it. But did they apologise? Oh dear no.

"Another time. One morning at breakfast. Martha didn't like her raspberry vinegar. So she didn't drink it. And Simon came into the nursery. And he saw that Martha hadn't drunk her raspberry vinegar. And he asked her why. And she said she didn't like it. Because it was nasty. And he said it wasn't nasty. And that she *ought* to like it. And how it was shocking. The way grown-ups nowadays grumbled. At good wholesome food. Provided for them by their too-indulgent children. And how when *he* was a grown-up. He would never have dared. And so on. All in the usual style. And to prove it wasn't nasty. He poured himself out a cupful. And drank it off. In a gulp. And he said it was delicious. And turned pale. And left the room.

"And Prue came into the nursery. And she saw that Martha hadn't drunk her raspberry vinegar. And she asked her why. And Martha told her how she didn't like it. Because it was nasty. And Prue told her she ought to be ashamed of herself. For not liking it. Because it was good for her. And really very nice. And anyhow she'd *got* to like it. And not get stuffing herself up with messy tea and coffee. Because she wouldn't have it. And there was an end of it. And so on. And to prove it was all right. She poured herself out a cupful. And drank it off. In a gulp. And she said there was nothing wrong with it. Nothing whatever. And turned pale. And left the room.

"And it wasn't raspberry vinegar. But just red ink. What had got put into the raspberry vinegar decanter. By an oversight. And they needn't have been ill at all. If only they had listened. To poor old Martha. But no. That was their fixed idea. That grown-ups hadn't any sense. At all. What is a mistake. As one perceives."

Other characters had been sketched, some of them to be abandoned after a few bold touches: the difficulty of avoiding too close a portraiture to the living original having apparently proved irksome. Against one such, evidently an attempt to help Dick see himself in his true colours, I find this marginal, note in pencil: "Better not. Might make him ratty." Opposite to another—obviously of Mrs. St. Leonard, and with instinct for alliteration—is scribbled; "Too terribly true. She'd twig it."

Another character is that of a gent: "With a certain gift. For telling stories. Some of them *not bad*." A promising party, on the whole. Indeed, one might say, judging from description, a quite rational person: "*When not on the rantan*. But inconsistent." He is the grown-up of a little girl: "Not beautiful. But strangely attractive. Whom we will call Enid." One gathers that if all the children had been Enids, then surely the last word in worlds had been said. She has only this one grown-up of her very own; but she makes it her business to adopt and reform all the incorrigible old folk the other children have despaired of. It is all done by kindness. "She is *ever* patient. And just." Prominent among her numerous *protégées* is a military man, an elderly colonel; until she took him in hand, the awful example of what a grown-up might easily become, left to the care of incompetent infants. He defies his own child, a virtuous youth, but "lacking in sympathy;" is rude to his little nephews and nieces; a holy terror to his governess. He uses wicked words, picked up from retired pirates. "Of course without understanding. Their terrible significance." He steals the Indian's fire-water. "What few can partake of. With impunity." Certainly not the Colonel. "Can this be he! This gibbering wreck!" He hides cigars in a hollow tree, and smokes on the sly. He plays truant. Lures other old gentlemen away from their lessons to join him. They are discovered in the woods, in a cave, playing whist for sixpenny points.

Does Enid storm and bullyrag; threaten that if ever she catches him so much as looking at a card again she will go straight out and tell the dragon, who will in his turn be so shocked that in all probability he will decide on coming back with her to kill and eat the Colonel on the spot? No. "Such are not her methods." Instead she smiles: "indulgently." She says it is only natural for grown-ups to like playing cards. She is not angry with him. And there is no need for him to run away and hide in a nasty damp cave. "*She herself will play whist with him.*" The effect upon the Colonel is immediate: he bursts into tears. She plays whist with him in the garden: "After school hours. When he has been *good*." Double dummy, one presumes. One leaves the Colonel, in the end, cured of his passion for whist. Whether as the consequence of her play or her influence the "Rough Notes" give no indication.

In the play, I am inclined to think, Veronica received assistance. The house had got itself finished early in September. Young Bute has certainly done wonders. We performed it in the empty billiard-room, followed by a one-act piece of my own. The occasion did duty as a house-warming. We had quite a crowd, and ended up with a dance. Everybody seemed to enjoy themselves, except young Bertie St. Leonard, who played the Prince, and could not get out of his helmet in time for supper. It was a good helmet, but had been fastened clumsily; and inexperienced people trying to help had only succeeded in jambing all the screws. Not only wouldn't it come off, it would not even open for a drink. All thought it an excellent joke, with the exception of young Herbert St. Leonard. Our Mayor, a cheerful little man and very popular, said that it ought to be sent to *Punch*. The local reporter reminded him that the late John Leech had already made use of precisely the same incident for a comic illustration, afterwards remembering that it was not Leech, but the late Phil May. He seemed to think this ended the matter. St. Leonard and the Vicar, who are rival authorities upon the subject, fell into an argument upon armour in general, with special reference to the fourteenth century. Each used the boy's head to confirm his own theory, passing it triumphantly from one to the other. We had to send off young Hopkins in the donkey-cart for the blacksmith. I have found out, by the way, how it is young Hopkins makes our donkey go. Young Hopkins argues it is far less brutal than whacking him, especially after experience has proved that he evidently does not know why you are whacking him. I am not at all sure the boy is not right.

Janie played the Fairy Godmamma in a white wig and panniers. She will make a beautiful old lady. The white hair gives her the one thing that she lacks: distinction. I found myself glancing apprehensively round the room, wishing we had not invited so many eligible bachelors. Dick is making me anxious. The sense of his own unworthiness, which has come to him quite suddenly, and apparently with all the shock of a new discovery, has completely unnerved him. It is a healthy sentiment, and does him good. But I do not want it carried to the length of losing her. The thought of what he might one day bring home has been a nightmare to me ever since he left school. I suppose it is to most fathers. Especially if one thinks of the women one loved oneself when in the early twenties. A large pale-faced girl, who served in a bun-shop in the Strand, is the first I can recollect. How I trembled when by chance her hand touched mine! I cannot recall a single attraction about her except her size, yet for nearly six months I lunched off pastry and mineral waters merely to be near her. To this very day an attack of indigestion will always recreate her image in my mind. Another was a thin, sallow girl, but with magnificent eyes, I met one afternoon in the South Kensington Museum. She was a brainless, vixenish girl, but the memory of her eyes would always draw me back to her. More than two-thirds of our time together we spent in violent quarrels; and all my hopes of eternity I would have given to make her my companion for life. But for Luck, in the shape of a well-to-do cab proprietor, as great an idiot as myself I might have done it. The third was a chorus girl: on the whole, the best of the bunch. Her father was a coachman, and she had ten brothers and sisters, most of them doing well in service. And she was succeeded—if I have the order correct—by the ex-wife of a solicitor, a sprightly lady; according to her own account the victim of complicated injustice. I daresay there were others, if I took the time to think; but not one of them can I remember without returning thanks to Providence for having lost her. What is one to do? There are days in springtime when a young man ought not to be allowed outside the house. Thank Heaven and Convention it is not the girls who propose! Few women, who would choose the right moment to put their hands upon a young man's shoulders, and, looking into his eyes, ask him to marry them next week, would receive No for an answer. It is only our shyness that saves us. A wise friend of mine, who has observed much, would have all those marrying under five-and-twenty divorced by automatic effluxion of time at forty, leaving the few who had chosen satisfactorily to be reunited if they wished: his argument being that to condemn grown men and women to abide by the choice of inexperienced boys and girls is unjust and absurd. There were nice girls I could have fallen in love with. They never occurred to me. It would seem as if a man had to learn taste in women as in all other things, namely, by education. Here and there may exist the born connoisseur. But with most of us our first instincts are towards vulgarity. It is Barrie, I think, who says that if only there were silly women enough to go round, good women would never get a look in. It is certainly remarkable, the number of sweet old maids one meets. Almost as remarkable as the number of stupid, cross-grained wives. As I tell Dick, I have no desire for a daughter-in-law of whom he feels himself worthy. If he can't do better than that he had best remain single. Janie and he, if I know anything of life, are just suited for one another. Helpful people take their happiness in helping. I knew just such another, once: a sweet, industrious, sensible girl. She made the mistake of marrying a thoroughly good man. There was nothing for her to do. She ended by losing all interest in him, devoting herself to a Home in the East End for the reformation of newsboys. It was a pitiful waste: so many women would have been glad of him; while to the ordinary sinful man she would have been a life-long comfort. I must have a serious talk to Dick. I shall point out what a good thing it will be for her. I can see Dick keeping her busy and contented for the rest of her days.

Veronica played the Princess,—with little boy Foy—"Sir Robert of the Curse"—as her page. Anything more dignified has, I should say, rarely been seen upon the English stage. Among her wedding presents were: Two Votes for Women, presented by the local Fire Brigade; a Flying Machine of "proved stability. Might be used as a bathing tent;" a National Theatre, "with Cold Water Douche in Basement for reception of English Dramatists;" Recipe for building a Navy, without paying for it, "Gift of that great Financial Expert, Sir Hocus Pocus;" one Conscientious Income Taxpayer, "has been driven by a Lady;"

two Socialists in agreement as to what it means, "smaller one slightly damaged;" one Contented Farmer, "Babylonian Period;" and one extra-sized bottle, "Solution of the Servant Problem."

Dick played the "Dragon without a Tail." We had to make him without a tail owing to the smallness of the stage. He had once had a tail. But that was a long story: added to which there was not time to tell it. Little Sally St. Leonard played his wife, and Robina was his mother-in-law. So much depends upon one's mood. What an ocean of boredom might be saved if science could but give us a barometer foretelling us our changes of temperament! How much more to our comfort we could plan our lives, knowing that on Monday, say, we should be feeling frivolous; on Saturday "dull to bad-tempered."

I took a man once to see *The Private Secretary*. I began by enjoying myself, and ended by feeling ashamed of myself and vexed with the scheme of creation. That authors should write such plays, that actors should be willing to degrade our common nature by appearing in them was explainable, he supposed, by the law of supply and demand. What he could not understand was how the public could contrive to extract amusement from them. What was there funny in seeing a poor gentleman shut up in a box? Why should everybody roar with laughter when he asked for a bun? People asked for buns every day—people in railway refreshment rooms, in aerated bread shops. Where was the joke? A month later I found myself by chance occupying the seat just behind him at the pantomime. The low comedian was bathing a baby, and tears of merriment were rolling down his cheeks. To me the whole business seemed painful and revolting. We were being asked to find delight in the spectacle of a father—scouring down an infant of tender years with a scrubbing-brush. How women—many of them mothers—could remain through such an exhibition without rising in protest appeared to me an argument against female suffrage. A lady entered, the wife, so the programme informed me, of a Baron! All I can say is that a more vulgar, less prepossessing female I never wish to meet. I even doubted her sobriety. She sat down plump upon the baby. She must have been a woman rising sixteen stone, and for one minute fifteen seconds by my watch the whole house rocked with laughter. That the thing was only a stage property I felt was no excuse. The humour—heaven save the mark—lay in the supposition that what we were witnessing was the agony and death—for no child could have survived that woman's weight—of a real baby. Had I been able to tap myself beforehand

I should have learned that on that particular Saturday I was going to be "set-serious." Instead of booking a seat for the pantomime I should have gone to a lecture on Egyptian pottery which was being given by a friend of mine at the London Library, and have had a good time.

Children could tap their parents, warn each other that father was "going down;" that mother next week was likely to be "gusty." Children themselves might hang out their little barometers. I remember a rainy day in a country house during the Christmas holidays. We had among us a Member of Parliament: a man of sunny disposition, extremely fond of children. He said it was awfully hard lines on the little beggars cooped up in a nursery; and borrowing his host's motor-coat, pretended he was a bear. He plodded round on his hands and knees and growled a good deal, and the children sat on the sofa and watched him. But they didn't seem to be enjoying it, not much; and after a quarter of an hour or so he noticed this himself. He thought it was, maybe, that they were tired of bears, and fancied that a whale might rouse them. He turned the table upside down and placed the children in it on three chairs, explaining to them that they were ship-wrecked sailors on a raft, and that they must be careful the whale did not get underneath it and upset them. He draped a sheet over the towel-horse to represent an iceberg, and rolled himself up in a mackintosh and flopped about the floor on his stomach, butting his head occasionally against the table in order to suggest to them their danger. The attitude of the children still remained that of polite spectators. True, the youngest boy did make the suggestion of borrowing the kitchen toasting-fork, and employing it as a harpoon; but even this appeared to be the outcome rather of a desire to please than of any warmer interest; and, the whale objecting, the idea fell through. After that he climbed up on the dresser and announced to them that he was an ourang-outang. They watched him break a soup-tureen, and then the eldest boy, stepping out into the middle of the room, held up his arm, and the Member of Parliament, somewhat surprised, sat down on the dresser and listened.

"Please, sir," said the eldest boy, "we're awfully sorry. It's awfully good of you, sir. But somehow we're not feeling in the mood for wild beasts this afternoon."

The Member of Parliament brought them down into the drawing-room, where we had music; and the children, at their own request, were allowed to sing hymns. The next day they came of their own accord, and asked the Member of Parliament to play at beasts with them; but it seemed he had letters to write.

There are times when jokes about mothers-in-law strike me as lacking both in taste and freshness. On this particular evening they came to me bringing with them all the fragrance of the days that are no more. The first play I ever saw dealt with the subject of the mother-in-law—the "Problem" I think it was called in those days. The occasion was an amateur performance given in aid of the local Ragged School. A cousin of mine, lately married, played the wife; and my aunt, I remember, got up and walked out in the middle of the second act. Robina, in spectacles and an early Victorian bonnet, reminded me of her. Young Bute played a comic cabman. It was at the old Haymarket, in Buckstone's time, that I first met the cabman of art and literature. Dear bibulous, becoated creature, with ever-wrathful outstretched palm and husky "'Ere! Wot's this?" How good it was to see him once again! I felt I wanted to climb over the foot-lights and shake him by the hand. The twins played a couple of Young Turks, much concerned about their constitutions; and made quite a hit with a topical duet to the refrain: "And so you see The reason he Is not the Boss for us." We all agreed it was a pun worthy of Tom Hood himself. The Vicar thought he had heard it before, but this seemed improbable. There was a unanimous call for Author, giving rise to sounds of discussion behind the curtain. Eventually the whole company appeared, with Veronica in the centre. I had noticed throughout that the centre of the stage appeared to be Veronica's favourite spot. I can see the makings of a leading actress in Veronica.

In my own piece, which followed, Robina and Bute played a young married couple who do not know how to quarrel. It has always struck me how much more satisfactorily people quarrel on the stage than in real life. On the stage the man, having made up his mind—to have it out, enters and closes the door. He lights a cigarette; if not a teetotaller mixes himself a brandy-and-soda. His wife all this time is careful to remain silent. Quite evident it is that he is preparing for her benefit something unpleasant, and chatter might disturb him. To fill up the time she toys with a novel or touches softly the keys of the piano until he is quite comfortable and ready to begin. He glides into his subject with the studied calm of one with all the afternoon before him. She listens to him in rapt attention. She does not dream of interrupting him; would scorn the suggestion of chipping in with any little notion of her own likely to disarrange his train of thought. All she does when he pauses, as occasionally he has to for the purpose of taking breath, is to come to his assistance with short encouraging remarks, such, for instance, as: "Well." "You think that." "And if I did?" Her object seems to be to help him on. "Go on," she says from time to time, bitterly. And he goes on. Towards the end, when he shows signs of easing up, she puts it to him as one sportsman to another: Is he quite finished? Is that all? Sometimes it isn't. As often as not he has been saving the pick of the basket for the last.

"No," he says, "that is not all. There is something else!"

That is quite enough for her. That is all she wanted to know. She merely asked in case there might be. As it appears there is, she re-settles herself in her chair and is again all ears.

When it does come—when he is quite sure there is nothing he has forgotten, no little point that he has overlooked, she rises.

"I have listened patiently," she begins, "to all that you have said." (The devil himself could not deny this. "Patience" hardly seems the word. "Enthusiastically" she might almost have said). "Now"—with rising inflection—"you listen to me."

The stage husband—always the gentleman—bows;—stiffly maybe, but quite politely; and prepares in his turn to occupy the *rôle* of dumb but dignified defendant. To emphasise the coming change in their positions, the lady most probably crosses over to what has hitherto been his side of the stage; while he, starting at the same moment, and passing her about the centre, settles himself down in what must be regarded as the listener's end of the room. We then have the whole story over again from her point of view; and this time it is the gentleman who would bite off his tongue rather than make a retort calculated to put the lady off.

In the end it is the party who is in the right that conquers. Off the stage this is more or less of a toss-up; on the stage, never. If justice be with the husband, then it is his voice that, gradually growing louder and louder, rings at last triumphant through the house. The lady sees herself that she has been to blame, and wonders why it did not occur to her before—is grateful for the revelation, and asks to be forgiven. If, on the other hand, it was the husband who was at fault, then it is the lady who will be found eventually occupying the centre of the stage; the miserable husband who, morally speaking, will be trying to get under the table.

Now, in real life things don't happen quite like this. What the quarrel in real life suffers from is want of system. There is no order, no settled plan. There is much too much go-as-you-please about the quarrel in real life, and the result is naturally pure muddle. The man, turning things over in the morning while shaving, makes up his mind to have this matter out and have done with it. He knows exactly what he is going to say. He repeats it to himself at intervals during the day. He will first say This, and then he will go on to That; while he is about it he will perhaps mention the Other. He reckons it will take him a quarter of an hour. Which will just give him time to dress for dinner.

After it is over, and he looks at his watch, he finds it has taken him longer than that. Added to which he has said next to nothing—next to nothing, that is, of what he meant to say. It went wrong from the very start. As a matter of fact there wasn't any start. He entered the room and closed the door. That is as far as he got. The cigarette he never even lighted. There ought to have been a box of matches on the mantelpiece behind the photo-frame. And of course there were none there. For her to fly into a temper merely because he reminded her that he had spoken about this very matter at least a hundred times before, and accuse him of going about his own house "stealing" his own matches was positively laughable. They had quarrelled for about five minutes over those wretched matches, and then for another ten because he said that women had no sense of humour, and she wanted to know how he knew. After that there had cropped up the last quarter's gas-bill, and that by a process still mysterious to him had led them into the subject of his behaviour on the night of the Hockey Club dance. By an effort of almost supernatural self-control he had contrived at length to introduce the subject he had come home half an hour earlier than usual on purpose to discuss. It didn't interest her in the least. What she was full of by this time was a girl named Arabella Jones. She got in quite a lot while he was vainly trying to remember where he had last seen the damned girl. He had just succeeded in getting back to his own topic when the Cuddiford girl from next door dashed in without a hat to borrow a tuning-fork. It had been quite a business finding the tuning-fork, and when she was gone they had to begin all over again. They had quarrelled about the drawing-room carpet; about her sister Florrie's birthday present; and the way he drove the motor-car. It had taken them over an hour and a half, and rather than waste the tickets for the theatre, they

JEROME K. JEROME

had gone without their dinner. The matter of the cold chisel still remained to be thrashed out.

It had occurred to me that through the medium of the drama I might show how the domestic quarrel could so easily be improved. Adolphus Goodbody, a worthy young man deeply attached to his wife, feels nevertheless that the dinners she is inflicting upon him are threatening with permanent damage his digestive system. He determines, come what may, to insist upon a change. Elvira Goodbody, a charming girl, admiring and devoted to her husband, is notwithstanding a trifle *en tête*, especially when her domestic arrangements happen to be the theme of discussion. Adolphus, his courage screwed to the sticking-point, broaches the difficult subject; and for the first half of the act my aim was to picture the progress of the human quarrel, not as it should be, but as it is. They never reach the cook. The first mention of the word "dinner" reminds Elvira (quick to perceive that argument is brewing, and alive to the advantage of getting in first) that twice the month before he had dined out, not returning till the small hours of the morning. What she wants to know is where this sort of thing is going to end? If the purpose of Freemasonry is the ruin of the home and the desertion of women, then all she has to say—it turns out to be quite a good deal. Adolphus, when able to get in a word, suggests that eleven o'clock at the latest can hardly be described as the "small hours of the morning": the fault with women is that they never will confine themselves to the simple truth. From that point onwards, as can be imagined, the scene almost wrote itself. They have passed through all the customary stages, and are planning, with exaggerated calm, arrangements for the separation which each now feels to be inevitable, when a knock comes to the front-door, and there enters a mutual friend.

Their hasty attempts to cover up the traces of mental disorder with which the atmosphere is strewed do not deceive him. There has been, let us say, a ripple on the waters of perfect agreement. Come! What was it all about?

"About!" They look from one to the other. Surely it would be simpler to tell him what it had *not* been about. It had been about the parrot, about her want of punctuality, about his using the butter-knife for the marmalade, about a pair of slippers he had lost at Christmas, about the education question, and her dressmaker's bill, and his friend George, and the next-door dog—

The mutual friend cuts short the catalogue. Clearly there is nothing for it but to begin the quarrel all over again; and this time, if they will put themselves into his hands, he feels sure he can promise victory to whichever one is in the right.

Elvira—she has a sweet, impulsive nature—throws her arms around him: that is all she wants. If only Adolphus could be brought to see! Adolphus grips him by the hand. If only Elvira would listen to sense!

The mutual friend—he is an old stage-manager—arranges the scene: Elvira in easy-chair by fire with crochet. Enter Adolphus. He lights a cigarette; flings the match on the floor; with his hands in his pockets paces up and down the room; kicks a footstool out of his way.

"Tell me when I am to begin," says Elvira.

The mutual friend promises to give her the right cue.

Adolphus comes to a halt in the centre of the room.

"I am sorry, my dear," he says, "but there is something I must say to you—something that may not be altogether pleasant for you to hear."

To which Elvira, still crocheting, replies, "Oh, indeed. And pray what may that be?"

This was not Elvira's own idea. Springing from her chair, she had got as far as: "Look here. If you have come home early merely for the purpose of making a row—" before the mutual friend could stop her. The mutual friend was firm. Only by exacting strict obedience could he guarantee a successful issue. What she had got to say was, "Oh, indeed. Etcetera." The mutual friend had need of all his tact to prevent its becoming a quarrel of three.

Adolphus, allowed to proceed, explained that the subject about which he wished to speak was the subject of dinner. The mutual friend this time was beforehand. Elvira's retort to that was: "Dinner! You complain of the dinners I provide for you?" enabling him to reply, "Yes, madam, I do complain," and to give reasons. It seemed to Elvira that the mutual friend had lost his senses. To tell her to "wait"; that "her time would come"; of what use was that! Half of what she wanted to say would be gone out of her head. Adolphus brought to a conclusion his criticism of Elvira's kitchen; and then Elvira, incapable of restraining herself further, rose majestically.

The mutual friend was saved the trouble of suppressing Adolphus. Until Elvira had finished Adolphus never got an opening. He grumbled at their dinners. He! who can dine night after night with his precious Freemasons. Does he think she likes them any better? She, doomed to stay at home and eat them. What does he take her for? An ostrich? Whose fault is it that they keep an incompetent cook too old to learn and too obstinate to want to? Whose old family servant was she? Not Elvira's. It has been to please Adolphus that she has suffered the woman. And this is her reward. This! She breaks down. Adolphus is astonished and troubled. Personally he never liked the woman. Faithful she may have been, but a cook never. His own idea, had he been consulted, would have been a small pension. Elvira falls upon his neck. Why did he not say so before? Adolphus presses her to his bosom. If only he had known! They promise the mutual friend never to quarrel again without his assistance.

The acting all round was quite good. Our curate, who is a bachelor, said it taught a lesson. Veronica had tears in her eyes. She whispered to me that she thought it beautiful. There is more in Veronica than people think.

I am sorry the house is finished. There is a proverb: "Fools build houses for wise men to live in." It depends upon what you are after. The fool gets the fun, and the wise men the bricks and mortar. I remember a whimsical story I picked up at the bookstall of the Gare de Lyon. I read it between Paris and Fontainebleau many years ago. Three friends, youthful Bohemians, smoking their pipes after the meagre dinner of a cheap restaurant in the Latin Quarter, fell to thinking of their poverty, of the long and bitter struggle that lay before them.

"My themes are so original," sighed the Musician. "It will take me a year of *fête* days to teach the public to understand them, even if ever I do succeed. And meanwhile I shall live unknown, neglected; watching the men without ideals passing me by in the race, splashed with the mud from their carriage-wheels as I beat the pavements with worn shoes. It is really a most unjust world."

"An abominable world," agreed the Poet. "But think of me! My case is far harder than yours. Your gift lies within you. Mine is to translate what lies around me; and that, for so far ahead as I can see, will always be the shadow side of life. To develop my genius to its fullest I need the sunshine of existence. My soul is being starved for lack of the beautiful things of life. A little of the wealth that vulgar people waste would make a great poet for France. It is not only of myself that I am thinking."

The Painter laughed. "I cannot soar to your heights," he said. "Frankly speaking, it is myself that chiefly appeals to me. Why not? I give the world Beauty, and in return what does it give me? This dingy restaurant, where I eat ill-flavoured food off hideous platters, a foul garret giving on to chimney-pots. After long years of ill-requited labour I may—as others have before me—come into my kingdom: possess my studio in the Champs Elysées, my fine house at Neuilly; but the prospect of the intervening period, I confess, appals me."

Absorbed in themselves, they had not noticed that a stranger, seated at a neighbouring table, had been listening with attention. He rose and, apologising with easy grace for intrusion into a conversation he could hardly have avoided overhearing, requested permission to be of service. The restaurant was dimly lighted; the three friends on entering had chosen its obscurest corner. The Stranger appeared to be well-dressed; his voice and bearing suggested the man of affairs;

his face—what feeble light there was being behind him—remained in shadow.

The three friends eyed him furtively: possibly some rich but eccentric patron of the arts; not beyond the bounds of speculation that he was acquainted with their work, had read the Poet's verses in one of the minor magazines, had stumbled upon some sketch of the Painter's while bargain-hunting among the dealers of the Quartier St. Antoine, been struck by the beauty of the Composer's Nocturne in F heard at some student's concert; having made enquiries concerning their haunts, had chosen this method of introducing himself. The young men made room for him with feelings of hope mingled with curiosity. The affable Stranger called for liqueurs, and handed round his cigar-case. And almost his first words brought them joy.

"Before we go further," said the smiling Stranger, "it is my pleasure to inform you that all three of you are destined to become great."

The liqueurs to their unaccustomed palates were proving potent. The Stranger's cigars were singularly aromatic. It seemed the most reasonable thing in the world that the Stranger should be thus able to foretell to them their future.

"Fame, fortune will be yours," continued the agreeable Stranger. "All things delightful will be to your hand: the adoration of women, the honour of men, the incense of Society, joys spiritual and material, beauteous surroundings, choice foods, all luxury and ease, the world your pleasure-ground."

The stained walls of the dingy restaurant were fading into space before the young men's eyes. They saw themselves as gods walking in the garden of their hearts' desires.

"But, alas," went on the Stranger—and with the first note of his changed voice the visions vanished, the dingy walls came back—"these things take time. You will, all three, be well past middle-age before you will reap the just reward of your toil and talents. Meanwhile—" the sympathetic Stranger shrugged his shoulders—"it is the old story: genius spending its youth battling for recognition against indifference, ridicule, envy; the spirit crushed by its sordid environment, the drab monotony of narrow days. There will be winter nights when you will tramp the streets, cold, hungry, forlorn; summer days when you will hide in your attics, ashamed of the sunlight on your ragged garments; chill dawns when you will watch wild-eyed the suffering of those you love, helpless by reason of your poverty to alleviate their pain."

The Stranger paused while the ancient waiter replenished the empty glasses. The three friends drank in silence.

"I propose," said the Stranger, with a pleasant laugh, "that we pass over this customary period of probation—that we skip the intervening years—arrive at once at our true destination."

The Stranger, leaning back in his chair, regarded the three friends with a smile they felt rather than saw. And something about the Stranger—they could not have told themselves what—made all things possible.

"A quite simple matter," the Stranger assured them. "A little sleep and a forgetting, and the years lie behind us. Come, gentlemen. Have I your consent?"

It seemed a question hardly needing answer. To escape at one stride the long, weary struggle; to enter without fighting into victory! The young men looked at one another. And each one, thinking of his gain, bartered the battle for the spoil.

It seemed to them that suddenly the lights went out; and a darkness like a rushing wind swept past them, filled with many sounds. And then forgetfulness. And then the coming back of light.

They were seated at a table, glittering with silver and dainty chinaware, to which the red wine in Venetian goblets, the varied fruit and flowers, gave colour. The room, furnished too gorgeously for taste, they judged to be a private cabinet in one of the great restaurants. Of such interiors they had occasionally caught glimpses through open windows on summer nights. It was softly illuminated by shaded lamps. The Stranger's face was still in shadow. But what surprised each of the three most was to observe opposite him two more or less bald-headed gentlemen of somewhat flabby appearance, whose features, however, in some mysterious way appeared familiar. The Stranger had his wine-glass raised in his hand.

"Our dear Paul," the Stranger was saying, "has declined, with his customary modesty, any public recognition of his triumph. He will not refuse three old friends the privilege of offering him their heartiest congratulations. Gentlemen, I drink not only to our dear Paul, but to the French Academy, which in honouring him has honoured France."

The Stranger, rising from his chair, turned his piercing eyes—the only part of him that could be clearly seen—upon the astonished Poet. The two elderly gentlemen opposite, evidently as bewildered as Paul himself, taking their cue from the Stranger, drained their glasses. Still following the Stranger's lead, leant each across the table and shook him warmly by the hand.

"I beg pardon," said the Poet, "but really I am afraid I must have been asleep. Would it sound rude to you"—he addressed himself to the Stranger: the faces of the elderly gentlemen opposite did not suggest their being of much assistance to him—"if I asked you where I was?"

Again there flickered across the Stranger's face the smile that was felt rather than seen. "You are in a private room of the Café Pretali," he answered. "We are met this evening to celebrate your recent elevation into the company of the Immortals."

"Oh," said the Poet, "thank you."

"The Academy," continued the Stranger, "is always a little late in these affairs. Myself, I could have wished your election had taken place ten years ago, when all France—all France that counts, that is— was talking of you. At fifty-three"—the Stranger touched lightly with his fingers the Poet's fat hand—"one does not write as when the sap was running up, instead of down."

Slowly, memory of the dingy *café* in the Rue St. Louis, of the strange happening that took place there that night when he was young, crept back into the Poet's brain.

"Would you mind," said the Poet, "would it be troubling you too much to tell me something of what has occurred to me?"

"Not in the least," responded the agreeable Stranger. "Your career has been most interesting—for the first few years chiefly to yourself. You married Marguerite. You remember Marguerite?"

The Poet remembered her.

"A mad thing to do, so most people would have said," continued the Stranger. "You had not a sou between you. But, myself, I think you were justified. Youth comes to us but once. And at twenty-five our business is to live. Undoubtedly the marriage helped you. You lived an idyllic existence, for a time, in a tumble-down cottage at Suresnes, with a garden that went down to the river. Poor, of course you were; poor as church mice. But who fears poverty when hope and love are singing on the bough! I really think quite your best work was done during those years at Suresnes. Ah, the sweetness, the tenderness of it! There has been nothing like it in French poetry. It made no mark at the time; but ten years later the public went mad about it. She was dead then. Poor child, it had been a hard struggle. And, as you may remember, she was always fragile. Yet even in her death I think she helped you. There entered a new note into your poetry, a depth that had hitherto been wanting. It was the best thing that ever came to you, your love for Marguerite."

The Stranger refilled his glass, and passed the decanter. But the Poet left the wine unheeded.

"And then, ah, yes, then followed that excursion into politics. Those scathing articles you wrote for *La Liberté*! It is hardly an exaggeration to say that they altered the whole aspect of French political thought. Those wonderful speeches you made during your election campaign at Angers. How the people worshipped you! You might have carried your portfolio had you persisted. But you poets are such restless fellows. And after all, I daresay you have really accomplished more by your plays. You remember—no, of course, how could you?—the first night of *La Conquête*. Shall I ever forget it! I have always reckoned that the crown of your career. Your marriage with Madame Deschenelle—I do not think it was for the public good. Poor Deschenelle's millions—is it not so? Poetry and millions interfere with one another. But a thousand pardons, my dear Paul. You have done so much. It is only right you should now be taking your ease. Your work is finished."

The Poet does not answer. Sits staring before him with eyes turned inward. The Painter, the Musician: what did the years bring to them? The Stranger tells them also of all that they have lost: of the griefs and sorrows, of the hopes and fears they have never tasted, of their tears that ended in laughter, of the pain that gave sweetness to joy, of the triumphs that came to them in the days before triumph had lost its savour, of the loves and the longings and fervours they would never know. All was ended. The Stranger had given them what he had promised, what they had desired: the gain without the getting.

Then they break out.

"What is it to me," cries the Painter, "that I wake to find myself wearing the gold medal of the Salon, robbed of the memory of all by which it was earned?"

The Stranger points out to him that he is illogical; such memories would have included long vistas of meagre dinners in dingy restaurants, of attic studios, of a life the chief part of which had been passed amid ugly surroundings. It was to escape from all such that he had clamoured. The Poet is silent.

"I asked but for recognition," cries the Musician, "that men might listen to me; not for my music to be taken from me in exchange for the

JEROME K. JEROME

recompense of a successful tradesman. My inspiration is burnt out; I feel it. The music that once filled my soul is mute."

"It was born of the strife and anguish," the Stranger tells him, "of the loves that died, of the hopes that faded, of the beating of youth's wings against the bars of sorrow, of the glory and madness and torment called Life, of the struggle you shrank from facing."

The Poet takes up the tale.

"You have robbed us of Life," he cries. "You tell us of dead lips whose kisses we have never felt, of songs of victory sung to our deaf ears. You have taken our fires, you have left us but the ashes."

"The fires that scorch and sear," the Stranger adds, "the lips that cried in their pain, the victory bought of wounds."

"It is not yet too late," the Stranger tells them. "All this can be but a troubled dream, growing fainter with each waking moment. Will you buy back your Youth at the cost of ease? Will you buy back Life at the price of tears?"

They cry with one voice, "Give us back our Youth with its burdens, and a heart to bear them! Give us back Life with its mingled bitter and sweet!"

Then suddenly the Stranger stands revealed before them. They see that he is Life—Life born of battle, Life made strong by endeavour, Life learning song from suffering.

There follows more talk; which struck me, when I read the story, as a mistake; for all that he tells them they have now learnt: that life to be enjoyed must be lived; that victory to be sweet must be won.

They awake in the dingy *café* in the Rue St. Louis. The ancient waiter is piling up the chairs preparatory to closing the shutters. The Poet draws forth his small handful of coins; asks what is to pay. "Nothing," the waiter answers. A stranger who sat with them and talked awhile before they fell asleep has paid the bill. They look at one another, but no one speaks.

The streets are empty. A thin rain is falling. They turn up the collars of their coats; strike out into the night. And as their footsteps echo on the glistening pavement it comes to each of them that they are walking with a new, brave step.

I feel so sorry for Dick—for the tens of thousands of happy, healthy, cared-for lads of whom Dick is the type. There must be millions of youngsters in the world who have never known hunger, except as an appetiser to their dinner; who have never felt what it was to be tired, without the knowledge that a comfortable bed was awaiting them.

To the well-to-do man or woman life is one perpetual nursery. They are wakened in the morning—not too early, not till the nursery has been swept out and made ready, and the fire lighted—awakened gently with a cup of tea to give them strength and courage for this great business of getting up—awakened with whispered words, lest any sudden start should make their little heads ache—the blinds carefully arranged to exclude the naughty sun, which otherwise might shine into their little eyes and make them fretful. The water, with the nasty chill off, is put ready for them; they wash their little hands and faces, all by themselves! Then they are shaved and have their hair done; their little hands are manicured, their little corns cut for them. When they are neat and clean, they toddle into breakfast; they are shown into their little chairs, their little napkins handed to them; the nice food that is so good for them is put upon their little plates; the drink is poured out for them into their cups. If they want to play, there is the day nursery. They have only to tell kind nurse what game it is they fancy. The toys are at once brought out. The little gun is put into their hand; the little horse is dragged forth from its corner, their little feet carefully placed in the stirrups. The little ball and bat is taken from its box.

Or they will take the air, as the wise doctor has ordered. The little carriage will be ready in five minutes; the nice warm cloak is buttoned round them, the footstool placed beneath their feet, the cushion at their back.

The day is done. The games have been played; the toys have been taken from their tired hands, put back into the cupboard. The food that is so good for them, that makes them strong little men and women, has all been eaten. They have been dressed for going out into the pretty Park, undressed and dressed again for going out to tea with the little boys and girls next door; undressed and dressed again for the party. They have read their little book? have seen a little play, have looked at pretty pictures. The kind gentleman with the long hair has played the piano to them. They have danced. Their little feet are really quite tired. The footman brings them home. They are put into their little nighties. The candle is blown out, the nursery door is softly closed.

Now and again some restless little man, wearying of the smug nursery, will run out past the garden gate, and down the long white road; will find the North Pole or, failing that, the South Pole, or where the Nile rises, or how it feels to fly; will climb the Mountains of the

Moon—do anything, go anywhere, to escape from Nurse Civilisation's everlasting apron strings.

Or some queer little woman, wondering where the people come from, will run and run till she comes to the great town, watch in wonder the strange folk that sweat and groan—the peaceful nursery, with the toys, the pretty frocks never quite the same again to her.

But to the nineteen-twentieths of the well-to-do the world beyond the nursery is an unknown land. Terrible things occur out there to little men and women who have no pretty nursery to live in. People push and shove you about, will even tread on your toes if you are not careful. Out there is no kind, strong Nurse Bank-Balance to hold one's little hand, and see that no harm comes to one. Out there, one has to fight one's own battles. Often one is cold and hungry, out there.

One has to fend for oneself, out there; earn one's dinner before one eats it, never quite sure of the week after next. Terrible things take place, out there: strain and contest and fierce endeavour; the ways are full of dangers and surprises; folk go up, folk go down; you have to set your teeth and fight. Well-to-do little men and women shudder. Draw down the nursery blinds.

Robina had a little dog. It led the usual dog's life: slept in a basket on an eiderdown cushion, sheltered from any chance draught by silk curtains; its milk warmed and sweetened; its cosy chair reserved for it, in winter, near the fire; in summer, where the sun might reach it; its three meals a day that a gourmet might have eaten gladly; its very fleas taken off its hands.

And twice a year still extra care was needed, lest it should wantonly fling aside its days and nights of luxurious ease, claim its small share of the passion and pain that go to the making of dogs and men. For twice a year there came a wind, salt with the brine of earth's ceaseless tides, whispering to it of a wondrous land whose sharpest stones are sweeter than the silken cushions of all the world without.

One winter's night there was great commotion. Babette was nowhere to be found. We were living in the country, miles away from everywhere. "Babette, Babette," cried poor frenzied Robina; and for answer came only the laughter of the wind, pausing in his game of romps with the snow-flakes.

Next morning an old woman from the town four miles away brought back Babette at the end of a string. Oh, such a soaked, bedraggled Babette! The old woman had found her crouching in a doorway, a bewildered little heap of palpitating femininity; and, reading the address upon her collar, and may be scenting a not impossible reward, had thought she might as well earn it for herself.

Robina was shocked, disgusted. To think that Babette—dainty, petted, spoilt Babette—should have chosen of her own accord to go down into the mud and darkness of the vulgar town; to leave her curtained eiderdown to tramp the streets like any drab! Robina, to whom Babette had hitherto been the ideal dog, moved away to hide her tears of vexation. The old dame smiled. She had borne her good man eleven, so she told us. It had been a hard struggle, and some had gone down, and some were dead; but some, thank God, were doing well.

The old dame wished us good day; but as she turned to go an impulse seized her. She crossed to where Babette, ashamed, yet half defiant, sat a wet, woeful little image on the hearthrug, stooped and lifted the little creature in her thin, worn arms.

"It's trouble you've brought yourself," said the old dame. "You couldn't help it, could you?"

Babette's little pink tongue stole out.

"We understand, we know—we Mothers," they seemed to be saying to one another.

And so the two kissed.

I think the terrace will be my favourite spot. Ethelbertha thinks, too, that on sunny days she will like to sit there. From it, through an opening I have made in the trees, I can see the cottage just a mile away at the edge of the wood. Young Bute tells me it is the very place he has been looking for. Most of his time, of course, he has to pass in town, but his Fridays to Mondays he likes to spend in the country. Maybe I shall hand it over to him. St. Leonard's chimneys we can also see above the trees. Dick tells me he has quite made up his mind to become a farmer. He thinks it would be a good plan, for a beginning, to go into partnership with St. Leonard. It is not unlikely that St. Leonard's restless temperament may prompt him eventually to tire of farming. He has a brother in Canada doing well in the lumber business, and St. Leonard often talks of the advantages of the colonies to a man who is bringing up a large family. I shall be sorry to lose him as a neighbour; though I see the advantages, under certain possibilities, of Mrs. St. Leonard's address being Manitoba.

Veronica also thinks the terrace may come to be her favourite resting-place.

"I suppose," said Veronica, "that if anything was to happen to Robina, everything would fall on me."

"It would be a change, Veronica," I suggested. "Hitherto it is you who have done most of the falling."

"Suppose I've got to see about growing up," said Veronica.

The End

A Note About the Author

Jerome K. Jerome (1859–1927) was an English writer who grew up in a poverty-stricken family. After multiple bad investments and the untimely deaths of both parents, the clan struggled to make ends meet. The young Jerome was forced to drop out of school and work to support himself. During his downtime, he enjoyed the theatre and joined a local repertory troupe. He branched out and began writing essays, satires and many short stories. One of his earliest successes was *Idle Thoughts of an Idle Fellow* (1886) but his most famous work is *Three Men in a Boat* (1889).

A Note from the Publisher

Spanning many genres, from non-fiction essays to literature classics to children's books and lyric poetry, Mint Edition books showcase the master works of our time in a modern new package. The text is freshly typeset, is clean and easy to read, and features a new note about the author in each volume. Many books also include exclusive new introductory material. Every book boasts a striking new cover, which makes it as appropriate for collecting as it is for gift giving. Mint Edition books are only printed when a reader orders them, so natural resources are not wasted. We're proud that our books are never manufactured in excess and exist only in the exact quantity they need to be read and enjoyed.

Discover more of your favorite classics with Bookfinity™.

- Track your reading with custom book lists.
- Get great book recommendations for your personalized Reader Type.
- Add reviews for your favorite books.
- AND MUCH MORE!

Visit **bookfinity.com** and take the fun Reader Type quiz to get started.

Enjoy our classic and modern companion pairings!